the placebo effect trilogy

like blood in water

the future of giraffes

view of delft

What unites the three collections that make up *The Placebo Effect Trilogy* into a single novel-like structure are the themes that like motifs in music are repeated throughout them, binding them together the way characters and events in a traditional trilogy bind three separate novels into a unified work. In this the trilogy is like a complex musical composition, a symphony in three movements—a symphony of semantics rather than of sound. The unity of the work is further heightened by the form common to the three books—each of them consists of five *mininovels* which employ *negative text*—missing information the reader has to provide himself—that imparts the scope of novels to these short-story-sized texts.

The subject of the trilogy is life—the placebo effect of the empty sugar-coated pill of faith in the future encoded in the genes of every human being.

Like Blood in Water introduces the main themes which recur in the two subsequent books. These are alienation (all of the five mininovels, but in particular "Former Pianist Fitipaldo"), the scream as a manifestation of existential despair ("Screaming," "Pavarotti-Agamemnon"), loss of a child ("Screaming," "The Joys and Sorrows of R. York," "Pavarotti-Agamemnon"), and the fear of death (all five works).

The unifying topic in *The Future of Giraffes* is childhood. It is the subject of all five mininovels in the book. The first of them, "A Day in the Life," picks up the theme of screaming from the first book and introduces the theme of abandonment, a variant of the loss of a child, which reappears in the remaining four works, most vividly in the fourth mininovel, "The Quarry." The second mininovel, "The Short Unhappy Life of Pinky Schmuck," introduces the theme of departure from the norm (cognitive impairment) which is repeated in the third work, "Your Childhood," where it is presented in the form of albinism. The fifth mininovel, "Sunday Morning," whose main topic is abandonment, serves as the companion book-end to the first mininovel, the action in it taking place in physical surroundings substantially similar to those in the first.

All of the works in *View of Delft* contain German elements—characters, language, physical surroundings, textual allusions, and so forth—a theme introduced in the second book in "The Short Unhappy Life of Pinky Schmuck" and "Your Childhood." The themes of alienation and cognitive impairment are picked up in "The Idiot," the first work in the book. The subject of alienation is further treated in the next two mininovels, "Years of Travel" and "The Albino Syndrome." This latter work, as the title states, picks up the theme of albinism introduced in the second book which is a symbolic representation of the fear of death. (The fact the same character appears in the two works further strengthens the unity of the trilogy.) The topic of death is treated in the last three mininovels, "The Albino Syndrome," "Karla and Georg or the Ambiguous Nature of Clouds," and in particular "The School," where it is the main subject. The principal character in this work is named Rohark, which alludes to the principal character in the first work in *Like Blood in Water*, Roark, the two mininovels thus acting as book-ends to the trilogy. Both of these names, of course, have the word "roar' embedded in them, which is an emphatic equivalent of the word "scream."

yuriy tarnawsky

yuriy tarnawsky

view of delft
five mininovels

Journal of Experimental Fiction 53.3

JEF Books/Journal of Experimental Fiction/Depth Charge

Geneva, Illinois

The Placebo Effect Trilogy (ltd. edition boxed set)

ISBN 1-884097-53-7/ISBN-13 978-1-884097-53-9

Also published as *Journal of Experimental Fiction* 53

ISSN 1084-547X

Individual Volumes:

like blood in water

ISBN 1-884097-25-1/ISBN-13 978-1-884097-25-6

the future of giraffes

ISBN 1-884097-26-X/ISBN-13 978-1-884097-26-3

view of delft

ISBN 1-884097-27-8/ISBN-13 978-1-884097-27-0

Front Cover Art and Design: Norman Conquest

Book Design: Eckhard Gerdes

Typefaces: Goudy Old Style (body), PicturePostcard (headers)

Produced and Printed in the United States of America

"Karla and Georg or the Ambiguous Nature of Clouds" first published in Big Fiction Magazine, No. 1, 2011.

The foremost in innovative fiction

http://experimentalfiction.com

view of delft

five mininovels

For my wife Karina, although

she deserves much more

table of contents

the idiot

9

years of travel

63

the albino syndrome

113

karla and georg or the ambiguous nature of clouds

157

the school

189

the idiot

yurly tarnawsky || view of delft

To the memory of Ron Sukenick
before reading his Cows

1. moooooo

As Eugen Winter turned the corner and the little pond with its white diving tower which had always reminded him of the statue of the Winged Victory of Samothrace was about to emerge from behind the ugly blue house on his left he heard a loud mooing sound coming from behind his back on the right and, startled, since he never expected to come across a cow in the chic suburban surroundings he was finding himself in, he quickly turned his head in that direction.

His feet kept moving forward but as he caught sight of a pale squat shape next to a big rounded one on its right, concluding that what he saw was too unusual for him to let go unchecked and that if he continued walking he was in danger of stumbling and falling down, he stopped, turned around, and realized that he was looking at a male human figure about five feet tall, with wide hips, sloping shoulders, a small pointed head covered with thick, closely-cropped straw-yellow hair, a featureless pasty face, and pale eyes that even from that distance looked covered with a milky film.

Facing him some twenty feet away stood a boy about eighteen years old suffering from Down disease who stared at him intently while holding with his right hand onto a clump of flowers of the unusually luxuriant orange aster bush that reached up to his waist.

As Eugen Winter turned, the boy opened his mouth and made a long mooing sound that was an uncannily skillful imitation of the mooing of a cow—it was deep and long and ended with the kind of an abrupt break the sounds cows make always do which is probably caused by the peculiarities of their anatomy and which humans typically make no attempt at rendering, being apparently unaware of it.

A pleasant warm feeling as if from swallowing a mouthful of melted butter spread through Eugen Winter's chest and, his face relaxing and distending in a broad smile not unlike a puddle of melted butter spreading on a flat surface, he stepped forward.

Hello there, Eugen Winter said in a cooing voice as he would have to a calf that had mooed at him trying to attract his attention.

How are we doing this morning? He continued as he walked toward the boy and the latter remained standing in the same position staring mutely and waiting for him to come up.

You sound just like a cow, Eugen Winter said in an admiring way as he stopped a few feet away from the boy.

Huh, huh, huh, replied the boy, suddenly animated, shifting his weight from one foot to the other like a dancing bear on a tight chain, unable to move freely.

Bah, bah, bah, bah, he went on incomprehensibly in his nasal twang as he stepped up to Eugen Winter, grabbed the latter's right hand with his left, and pulled him toward the house that sat low behind the outline of the sloping, lush green lawn at the end of a slate walkway that bent in an esthetically pleasing way first to the right then to the left and then to the right again, running between two rows of flower bushes of various bright colors—red, maroon, purple, yellow—as luxuriant as the asters the boy had been holding onto of which they were a part. It was built in the Tudor style and had a tall slate roof, a sturdy, arched oak door, and big iron-framed casement windows.

Eugen Winter had always admired the house on his daily morning walks wondering what lay inside its walls and as he let himself be pulled by the boy now realized he was about to find that out. As he walked he was surprised to discover that his hand was no longer being held by the boy but that it was he who was clutching that of the latter. It was small and soft, feeling, as he remarked, probably very much like the clump of flowers the boy held in his hand as he watched him—Eugen Winter—walking down the street. A strong smell of warm milk wafted from the boy and Eugen Winter found it soothing as a strong soporific so that he could barely resist the desire to close his eyes and drift off into sleep.

2. phil and babs

The sloping of the lawn continued inside the house and four or five steps led from the landing on the inside of the front door to a sunken living room with many sofas, armchairs, coffee and lamp tables distributed over the oriental rugs that covered the floor almost as if in the showroom of a furniture store. The furniture, perhaps partly because of the legs that were part of it, looked like cattle or sheep grazing peacefully on the thick rugs.

Two persons sat in two different spots in the room far away from each other as if strangers or even enemies—a man and a woman, both middle-aged, the first in a woven African chair with a high fan-like back, and the second in a dainty French-provincial one with gracefully carved legs and arm rests. Neither of them rose as

Eugen Winter with the boy at his side came up to the edge of the landing.

Hello there, said the woman smiling warmly while looking at Eugen Winter. We're Gene's parents. "Gene" was obviously the boy's name.

He's been wanting to meet you ever since we moved here last month, said the man in an equally warm voice although with just a barely visible trace of a smile in it—more of one that has passed than which is still to come. He's watched you walking by every morning through the window and today had worked up his courage and went outside to wait for you.

He was up at daybreak, the woman took over from the man, He was so excited.

Eugen Winter searched for the proper words to answer the people with but was unable to come with suitable ones in his embarrassment at being the object of their attention and even more of the boy's admiration.

What's your name? Asked the woman after a longish pause Eugen Winter was unable to fill.

Oygen Veenter, Eugen Winter replied quickly, glad the woman had come to his rescue with a note of gratitude for her in his voice. It's German for "Eugene Winter." I was born in this country but my parents were German and they insisted on the German pronunciation of my first name and our surname.

Oh, it's wonderful that your name is Eugene, said the woman, The same as our son's.

He must have sensed it, the man intruded. He has extraordinary extrasensory capabilities... felt like you were like his brother.

His alter ego... himself, the woman corrected the man for obvious reasons.

Yes, of course... his alter ego, the man agreed, seeing his wife's point.

We're Phil and Babs, he added. We teach husbandry at a university.

Our last name is also German and it is spelled "S-o-m-m-e-r", the woman once again took over from her husband, But we pronounce it "Summer" because that's what it means in English.

Genius—that's what we call him, explained the woman, Genius must have sensed it's close to yours, and then added laughing, But ours is a lot warmer. And then they all laughed together like one big happy family, the boy with a series of loud laryngeal huh, huh, huhs.

3. bible

It is evening. Eugen Winter has come home from work, he prepares and eats his supper, does the dishes, sits down on the sofa in his living room planning to relax, when the madness in the apartment upstairs starts up again. He has moved to this place two months ago and things have been reasonably quiet at first but during the last two weeks it has gotten impossible. Practically every night, come eight o'clock or so, the guy in the apartment, a young Vietnamese, starts playing loud music, the floor creaks, and there are sounds of feet scraping and stomping. Clearly people are dancing. People are also coming and going to the apartment all the time and you can hear the door being opened and closed and the traffic on the staircase. Something must have changed because it was not like that before. He can't find an explanation for it.

Eugen Winter is beside himself. He lived in an unacceptable place before and was glad to find this one but it has turned out even worse.

He gets up, walks around a little, but that doesn't help. He is more roiled up inside than before. He has to control himself. He must learn to triumph over his body and surroundings. He lies down on the sofa, stretches out, closes his eyes, and crosses his arms on his chest. He immediately realizes the symbolism of this, quickly uncrosses his arms, lays them alongside his body, and tries to channel his thoughts into a peaceful current.

The music upstairs blares, feet scrape the floor, it creaks, from time to time someone stomps his or her foot hard which is even worse than if it were being done all the time. He cannot ignore it. It is like trying to relax under an elevated highway along which cars travel all the time. The dancing is taking place practically in his living room!

He feels like crying out of pity for himself because there is nothing he can do. He has banged on the ceiling and complained to the man before but this didn't help. Nobody hears the banging and the ruckus may stop for a few minutes after he talks to the man but then it starts up again and goes on as before. Neither the apartment management nor the police want to get involved in the dispute and there is no solution to it.

Then he thinks of the Bible. It lies on the end table next to the sofa and he can reach it without getting up. He picks it up, opens it, and reads.

Right away the words draw him in like streets that lead to another, peaceful location far away from the unbearable reality, each in its own direction, but ultimately all to the same quiet place. Soon he is there, in the world of the text. He reads on, gets to about three quarters down the page, when he notices the noise upstairs has stooped. Not a sound is heard coming from the apartment as if everyone had left. Eugen Winter is first surprised and then worried. Is he hearing right? Have the music and dancing really stopped or is he just imagining it? And if they have stopped is it for good or will they come back in a minute? He is afraid it is the latter. But the silence continues. People have either left the apartment without his hearing them or they have gone to sleep. Perhaps there is an orgy taking place upstairs and people are quiet having sex. After they are finished the noise will start up again. The silence goes on however and he decides not to worry but take advantage of it. He is tired and will go to sleep hoping the noise won't come back that night.

Eugen Winter uses the sofa for sleeping since he has turned the bedroom into his study. He makes his bed, undresses, puts on his sleep clothes, washes up, turns out the light, and goes to sleep. The apartment upstairs stays dead quiet all night and he gets a wonderful night's sleep as he hadn't for a long time. Reading the Bible has worked!

Eugen Winter wonders if the Bible has had a permanent effect but the next night, when eighth o'clock comes, the music starts up again, gradually accompanied more and more by the sound of dancing feet. For a while he tries to cope with the noise on his own, "in a natural way," as he describes it to himself, not wanting to overuse the Bible so as to resort to it at a more critical moment as if it would get worn out by too frequent use, but eventually he is unable to stand the noise and starts reading in the book. He reads a page, then another one, and then one more, but it has no effect. He grows despondent. He thought he had found a sure way of remedying his situation but it turns out not to be true. He concludes reluctantly that it was naive of him to think this would be a fail-proof method for stopping the noise and that the Bible wasn't meant to be used for such trivial purposes. Yet as he reads on he does calm down and in the end concludes that what had happened the previous night was a sign for him to turn to the Bible as a way of helping himself cope with the situation. The stopping of the noise was a way of turning him on to reading the

Bible. He agrees this is a fair deal, goes on reading, and is able to largely ignore the noise. Around ten o'clock the noise upstairs stops and he is able to spend a peaceful night. Sometimes the noise had stopped at around that time before but usually it went on much longer and Eugen Winter thinks that perhaps the Bible has helped this time too except in a less dramatic way—"naturally" as he once more describes it to himself. He again feels it is a fair deal and decides he has found a way of coping with his situation. The Bible has not let him down.

He resorts to reading in the Bible from then on whenever he absolutely can't stand the noise and on the whole feels his situation has improved. He can tolerate the noise better and it sometimes stops quite early and seldom goes on as late as it used to.

Eugen Winter resigns himself to living on like this but then one day realizes there hasn't been any noise in the apartment for almost a week. Such a thing has never happened before. He hasn't been reading in the Bible during all this time so, as a precautionary measure, in order to insure that the noise doesn't come back and more importantly that the technique works in the future, he reads in it that night. He does the same the following night, and then the one after that.

When there is no noise on the fourth night he doesn't read in the Bible but the noise still doesn't come back. From then on he starts skipping days and eventually even two at a time between the readings. Still there is no noise. He concludes the Vietnamese man must have gone away, perhaps to visit his home country. He has seen recently television programs about Vietnamese refugees revisiting Vietnam now that the political situation there has changed. He is sure this is what has happened in this case. The man went back to Vietnam to the place he was from to stay with his family. But sooner or later, he is sure, the man will return and the noise will start up again. He will have to rely then on the Bible as he had done in the past. He reads in the Bible from then on from time to time so as to preserve the pact he has established with it.

A few weeks go by but the man still hasn't come back and Eugen Winter has doubts about the vacation scenario. Maybe something else has happened—maybe the man has moved out. He thinks that would be too good to be true and is sure the truth will not be as nice.

Unexpectedly he meets the superintendent on the staircase that same day. He asks the man about the whereabouts of the Vietnamese guy from the floor above.

Hasn't he heard? The man asks. The guy was killed—had his throat slashed right in the apartment. Some friends or members of the family hadn't heard from him for a few days, so they contacted the management, the apartment was opened, and the man was found dead, lying in a pool of blood on the floor. The police were called in and an investigation was started. It turned out the guy was a drug dealer and had run afoul of somebody—a client, competitor, or partner. They had tried to keep the details of what happened away from the tenants so as not to frighten them and also in order not to scare prospective tenants away but he thought that by now everyone in the building knew about it. It happened more than a month ago.

No, he hasn't heard about it, Eugen Winter says. He keeps to himself and talks to hardly anyone in the building.

Yes, that has been observed, the superintendent remarks.

Eugen Winter is shocked. His nemesis has been killed! Is he himself the cause of it—his reading the Bible? The prospect is scary. It would mean he is a murderer. He didn't like the guy but he doesn't want to be the cause of anyone's death. But how could that be possible? The Bible is the good book, a book of love, so how could it have caused someone's death? The man was killed because he was a drug dealer and that is all. Many drug dealers end up this way. It is a coincidence that he himself was reading the Bible at the time to stop the noise the man was making.

The reasoning is sound and Eugen Winter calms down although qualms about his contributing to the man's death persist underneath the peace he has managed to restore to his mind.

That night he has a hard time falling asleep and tries not to lie on his back so as not to look at the ceiling. He keeps thinking of the blood on the floor in the apartment above and imagines it dripping down on him. When he does fall asleep in the end he dreams that blood drips from the ceiling on his hands crossed on his chest and that he can't move them away because he is tied down to the sofa. The dream doesn't leave him alone until the morning.

He wakes up at dawn weak as after a long illness. His hands feel sticky from the blood he has dreamed about and he has barely enough strength to get up and drag himself to the bathroom to wash them off. He looks like a ghost in the mirror with his pale face and circles under his eyes and can't imagine how he will go on living in the apartment. He doesn't want to look for another place but what else can he do?

Instinctively he thinks of reading the Bible but pushes the thought away as fast as he can. The Bible has done enough harm already. God knows what more damage it might do!

Then he has an idea—he will cover himself with something impermeable... a tarp or a plastic sheet. Maybe that will make him feel safer and the dream won't come back. A plastic sheet would be better because it is light. It wouldn't press down so hard on him. He decides red would be the best.

4. bedbugs

It had been an unusually hot summer which must have been conducive to bedbug breeding because as Eugen Winter would go on his daily strolls he could see them crawling up the walls of the buildings in long files—shiny brown rivulets that flowed up from the ground toward the windows and roofs. The sight was disgusting and he wondered what that would lead to.

In the fall there was a bedbug epidemic in much of the country. The media talked about nothing else but bedbugs and the government was taking measures to at least hold back the spread of the pest if not to stamp it out completely.

For a long time the building Eugen Winter lived in remained free of the insects and he was beginning to feel he would be one of the chosen few to escape the plight but it turned out not to be so. One day the bugs were in his building and the place was teeming with them. He would see them in the foyer, on the staircase, in the corridors, and of course his apartment. At night they bit him viciously and he would wake up in the morning scratching furiously covered all over with huge red welts.

It had been arranged for the building to be fumigated and schedules were being set up for various apartments to make the necessary steps for being ready. Some apartments had already been treated and Eugen Winter was waiting for a call or a knock on the door from the superintendent to make arrangements for his to be done.

He had recently purchased a computer, had installed it, it had worked properly, but then something happened and it wouldn't boot up. No manual had been provided with the computer as used to be in the past and the help program on the system was supposed to replace it. Since the computer wasn't working he was unable to access the program and he was beside himself with anger—what idiot would dream up for a device designed to help fixing a system to be available only when the system didn't need fixing? You had it when you didn't need it and didn't have it when you did!

He tried to contact the store where he had bought the computer but the line was always busy. Everyone was having problems with computers nowadays! So much for technological advances. He was reluctant to leave his apartment because he wanted to be available to make arrangements for the fumigator to come but in the end decided to do it. The store was just a few blocks away and he probably would be finished talking with the people sooner than if he had done it over the phone. He was most likely going to be called on the phone anyway so being away was no worse than for the phone to be busy. And if they did call him when he was away they would surely do it again and he would be back very soon so that nothing was going to be lost.

When he described the problem with the computer to the technician in the store he was told it was a hardware problem and he should bring the computer in to be serviced.

The computer had worked perfectly well for quite a while, he hadn't done anything to it physically, so a thought crossed Eugen Winter's mind that the problem might have something to do with the bedbug infestation. Perhaps they had crept into the computer and were interfering with its functioning.

Could that be the cause?

Well, the technician thought for a while. Perhaps.... They could have gotten inside the hard drive, causing it to malfunction, or the memory slots, perhaps dislodging one of the cards. This would certainly prevent the computer from operating properly. They hadn't had anyone with that particular problem so far but there was always the first time. He should bring the computer over and they would check it out.

If it turned out to be bedbugs it wouldn't be covered by the warranty however since the problem was externally caused.

Yes, Eugen Winter agreed readily, he understood that. He was willing to pay as much as necessary to have the computer fixed. He had gotten so used to having a computer—he used it for doing his accounting, scheduling, correspondence, etc., even his diary— that life without one was virtually impossible. He would bring the computer over later that day.

Calmed down he walked back home but when he opened the door to his apartment a strong unpleasant smell hit his nostrils and he saw a strange tall figure, all in black, moving about the apartment with a long stick in its hand.

At first he had no idea what it was—a vague association with creatures from outer space began forming itself in his mind—but then as he was just about to realize on his own what was happening the figure turned to him and with vigorous motions of its free arm indicated for him to leave. His place was being fumigated! The man was dressed head to toe in a black rubber suit, had a gas mask on his face, a canister on his back, and held the spray attachment in his hand.

Eugen Winter quickly stepped back into the corridor and shut the door.

He was shocked. They had gone into his apartment to fumigate it without letting him know! Now he wouldn't be able to get inside for at least twenty-four hours. How would he manage with only the clothes on his body and the piddling amount of money in his pocket? He had nowhere to stay and nothing to live on! They must have called him when he was away and since he wasn't there decided to fumigate the place anyway. How he would cope was no concern of theirs! But perhaps they didn't bother calling him at all—they just went to his door, knocked on it, and when no one answered let themselves in and went about their job.

He was boiling mad with anger and decided to look for the superintendent and give him a piece of his mind. How could they do something like that? It was their problem now and they had to solve it. Let them get him a hotel room for the night and feed him. Things like that must never be done. Here was another example of the incompetence that has pervaded the world just like the case with the help program on the computer.

He went looking for the superintendent but the man was nowhere to be found. Perhaps it wasn't his fault. Maybe he wasn't there and they just went into the apartment on their own. They were probably given the keys to the whole building.

To calm himself down Eugen Winter decided to take a walk. Thoughts ran in calmer currents in his mind after a while. He began formulating a plan. There was no point in his asking the management to put him up in a hotel. They would never do it. He had enough money for a couple of skimpy meals, so food wasn't a real problem. It would be good for him to go on a little diet. As to sleeping—he was reluctant to ask the couple of tenants he knew to let them spend the night at their place. He hardly ever spoke to them and besides they were on the same floor and probably also had had their places fumigated. Ask the superintendent to put him up in the boiler room? He wouldn't do that. Where would he sleep? On the floor? And besides it was probably against fire regulations. The best solution was his car. It was parked in the parking lot behind the building and he could sleep there without the danger of being attacked or bothered by the police. The seats in his car reclined, so he could sleep quite comfortably... practically as on his sofa. The car was the answer.

The only problem was he had left the car keys in his apartment. He kept his house keys and car keys separate so as not to carry too big a bunch of keys all the time. He hated them clinking and chafing in his pocket. But how could he get his car keys?

He would wait till the evening when the fumes in the apartment had settled down, would run inside quickly, and without breathing get the keys. He kept them in the drawer in his desk and it wouldn't take more than ten seconds for him to get them. He certainly could hold his breath that long. He had found a solution!

Relaxed completely he strolled through the streets and then went into a park and spent a few hours there. He was beginning to feel hungry but decided to wait for later. He would have his supper before going to sleep and then lunch the following day. By late afternoon he would be able to get inside his place.

Eugen Winter was going to wait till it got dark before fetching the car keys but he was getting tired of walking around and wanted to rest. He would stretch out in his car and listen to the radio and later have his supper. It was evening already and some five hours had passed since his place was fumigated, so he could risk rushing inside and getting the keys. Besides he wouldn't breathe anyway.

He stood before his door his heart pounding loudly. What if he breathed accidentally while inside? How dangerous was it? He decided to cover his mouth and nose with his handkerchief in case he happened to breathe. He did that, opened the door, and ran as quickly as he could inside. In a few seconds he was by the desk in his study, he opened the drawer, and searched with his hand for the keys. They were not there. His heart sank. He was in trouble. Where were they? He must have left them in the pants he wore the last time he drove. He thought he knew which pants those were. They hung on a hanger in the closet in the study. He ran quickly to its door, opened it, and looked for the pants. He found them, found one of the pockets, stuck his hand in it, and felt for the keys. They were not there. His heart sank again. Things were getting serious. He wanted to look for the other pocket but had a hard time finding it, so he felt with his hands on the outside to see if the keys were there. He couldn't feel them but this didn't mean they weren't there. It was easy to miss feeling something so small as a pair of car keys while being in a hurry. He started to look for the pocket and then realized he couldn't hold his breath any longer and breathed in. His hand wasn't pressed very tight against his mouth and nose and most if not all of the air got in past the handkerchief. It smelt horrible. Eugen Winter felt faint, not knowing if from lack of oxygen or the gas, or perhaps fear, and pressed the handkerchief tightly against his mouth and nose. He then breathed again because the first breath wasn't enough. The air still smelled horrible and he realized he couldn't last much longer like that. He either found the keys that very instant or he had to run out. The keys were probably in another pair of pants and he was about to identify the candidate for them when he decided he couldn't stay in the apartment any longer. He was either going to suffocate or poison himself. He had to run out. He turned around without closing the closet and rushed into the living room and then to the front door.

He fumbled as he tried to open the front door and in despair breathed in once more this time without the benefit of the handkerchief at all for his hand had moved away from his face. He nearly passed out at realizing what he had done. He was going to poison himself for sure!

He slammed the door shut once in the corridor and breathed in. The air still seemed to stink so he walked away from the door before resuming breathing. He had a hard time catching his breath and his heart pounded wildly in his chest seeming to jump around like a trapped bird. After quieting down a little he thought of his predicament. Where was he going to spend the night? Looking for the superintendent was pointless. How could the man help him? Then he thought of his car again. Break one of its windows and get inside? The idea was stupid. He already had enough problems with fixing his computer and now he would have to worry about the car. But how about sleeping under the car? It would protect him from the cold a little.... That too was stupid. How much protection could it provide? Besides it would be hard sleeping on bare asphalt and moreover, he recalled at the last moment, his car dripped oil so it would drip on him and stain his clothes.... No, that was not the answer. And what about the grass strip around the parking lot? It was at least soft. But he would be cold there too!

Then he had an idea which he realized instantly would work. He had a tent that he put up sometimes in his living room to sleep in, which stood rolled up in its case in a corner in the bathroom. He could get it and set it up on the grass strip in the parking lot. The bathroom was right by the front door and the door to it, he recalled vividly, was open. It would take him literally a few seconds to rush inside, grab the tent, and rush out again. He could do it even without pressing his handkerchief to his face.

There shouldn't be any need for him to breathe. He would leave the front door ajar so as not to have any problems opening it. And within that little time not that much air would escape into the corridor through a crack in the door.... Yes, that was the way to go and he would do it. He would wait a few minutes to catch his breath and then rush inside and get the tent. There were towels in the bathroom right next to the tent and he could grab them too and have something to sleep on and even cover himself with. He was pleased with himself. He had solved the problem and solved it well! He visualized the tent standing in its red case in the corner leaning against the wall ready to be taken.

5. fear and trembling

Eugen Winter is attending a therapy session of the type called Fear and Trembling. It is similar to the Primal Scream School of therapy and supposedly draws heavily on the practices of the Shaker religion.

The location the session is taking place at looks like a Quaker meeting house. It is spacious and airy, with large bare windows and plain functional furniture—pews occupying about two thirds of the hall.

It is in the open part of the hall that the session is conducted. The people are arranged in two circles, one within the other, each person facing a partner. There are between twenty and thirty people in each circle. The therapy consists of one of the persons in the pair making a face, gesticulating, screaming, and so on, with the goal of frightening the other person and making him/her shake with fear. This is supposed to get rid of people's phobias and other neuroses connected with being human. Once this is accomplished it is the other person's turn to do the same and the process is repeated. The outer circle then moves one place clockwise, so that each person has a new partner, and the process is repeated again.

Eugen Winter is in the outside circle and at this time faces an old man with gray hair and a gaunt emaciated face. The man messes up his own hair, places his index fingers next to the outside of his eyes, sticks the ring fingers of his hands in the corners of his mouth, pulls on the four fingers, sticks his tongue out, and growls. The man's eyes bulge, the inside of his lower eyelids are exposed, his teeth show, and his tongue hangs out between them. The effect of this is more comical than scary but Eugen Winter shakes as he is supposed to and pretends he is scared. He then does similar things with his face and makes a loud growling sound. The man cowers, pretending to be frightened, and Eugen

Winter moves one spot to his left. Every pair has completed its procedure.

This time Eugen Winter faces a young man somewhat taller than he. You are supposed to alternate between which person in the two circles starts first, so it is Eugen Winter's turn to go ahead. He gets up on his toes, raises his arms high up, points his fingers at the man like horns, makes a horrible face, and growls. The man pretends to be frightened, bends down, wraps his arms around himself, and shakes violently, making a plaintive whining noise. Eugen Winter stops, the man straightens up, gets up on his toes, makes an angry face, threatens Eugen Winter with his fists, and gives out a blood-curdling scream. The scream is very loud and the man's fists big, as a consequence Eugen Winter feels somewhat threatened, but the fear he pretends to feel is largely faked. Still he shakes violently and makes a muffled, guttural sound.

Eugen Winter's next partner is an older woman in her mid fifties, heavyset, with a puffy face and messy red hair. She pretends to want to scratch Eugen Winter's face and screams in a shrill, hysterical voice. Eugen Winter leans back, first protecting himself with his arms, and then shaking as hard as he can. He pretends to want to strangle the woman, growling through his teeth. She screams and shakes.

Things are moving gradually faster so that the session is beginning to look almost like a dance. Eugen Winter's partner is a young woman with curly brown hair and a moderately attractive thin pale face. She doesn't threaten Eugen Winter in any way but shakes herself, emitting a sound you make while feeling cold, Brrr! Eugen Winter shakes like she does and makes a similar Brrr sound. The woman smiles and repeats what she has just done except making the sound louder. Eugen Winter does the same, emitting a louder Brrr sound. They proceed doing this one after the other, moving gradually more back and forth and from side to side so that in the end they are effectively dancing. People around them and ultimately everyone in the two circles does the same so that now it really is one big group dance.

People seem to enjoy it a lot for they move faster and faster and make ever louder noises. They also shake more violently.

Eugen Winter shakes and says, Brrr, as loud as he can. He has lost his partner and is milling around in the crowd. Now everyone is doing the same. The light has gotten dimmer. The windows are in fact dark. It is night outside. Some of the windows are open and cold air streams in through them. It is very cold in the room. It looks as though this is why people are saying, Brrr, and move fast and shake so violently.

Eugen Winter realizes he does feel very cold himself. He shakes now naturally without forcing himself to do it. The cold is unbelievable. He tries to move as fast as he can but it doesn't help. Saying, Brrr, doesn't help either. He doesn't know what to do. He looks around to see what other people are doing but they are no longer there. They have all run away to save themselves from the cold. He is all alone. He feels desperate. He will freeze to death. What is he to do?

He wakes up and realizes the covers have slipped off the sofa onto the floor and he lies all exposed. It is cold in the room. He is shaking.

6. eugen winter moves in

Eugen Winter was installed in one of the garret rooms with sloping walls and windows recessed in deep alcoves. He decorated the room himself, painting the floor with its narrow wooden boards and distinct lines between them like those in a perspective drawing red and papering the walls with old newspapers he found stacked away in a trunk in a dark corner of the attic way under the roof. The old wooden bed, chest of drawers, table, and chair that were in the room he painted blue, green, red, and yellow respectively. For the windows Babs made curtains from old percale sheets with little blue periwinkle flower pattern on a white background which went well with the rest of the decor.

The first morning, when Eugen Winter woke up, staring him back in the face from the sloping wall was a terse little paragraph describing the murder of a landlady by a young grocery clerk, her lodger, which made him think of Dostoyevsky's *Crime and Punishment.* Was *he* another Rodion Raskolnikoff, a maladjusted young man languishing in his bleak garret room, a horrible crime brewing in his cold dark heart? He smiled blissfully—no! His situation was just the opposite. His room was white with the light filtering in through the thin curtains and the feeling in his chest was like warm milk.

Thinking on about men stuck in solitary rooms he remembered Rilke's *The Diary of Malte Laurids Brigge.* He recalled Rilke using the phrase "poor Malte" referring to his hero. Poor? He smiled again. No, he was anything but poor. The two flights of stairs that separated him from the street level made him two floors closer to seventh heaven. There were only five left to go!

Pushing the thoughts about the paragraph with the murder out of his mind he observed that it would stare him back in the face each morning most likely for the rest of his life but that it would in no way be capable of marring the happiness he had found. No blood would ever drip on him from it for he was no longer the kind of person whom blood spilled by someone else could stain.

For some reason a little ditty then came across his mind, one he had learned from his cousin Georg when he used to visit the latter on summer vacations in Germany years ago as a child. It was in German and went:

> *Auf dem Berg*
> *Da steht ein Kuh.*
> *Er macht den Aschloch*
> *Auf und zu.*

It meant:

> On the hill
> There stands a cow.
> It makes its asshole
> Go open and close.

He smiled again as he remembered the verse. Its unsophisticated, innocent vulgarity could not mar the feeling of happiness in his chest. It actually heightened it, waking up in him the innocence of childhood that had been asleep for years.

Two days later the two Eugenes celebrated their joint birthday—decades apart but on the same day and month, day of the week, and even hour—another example of the uncanny extrasensory talent of the young Gene. They had eggs baked in the ashes in the fireplace and pigeons roasted earlier over the fire stuffed with sparrows, stuffed with crickets, an improvised version of squab stuffed with larks, stuffed with grasshoppers, an old Roman recipe Phil had dug up somewhere, washed down with liberal servings of sweet red wine—another Roman practice, as Phil explained. The pigeons were caught in a square in front of a bank where they congregated by Eugen Winter under the watchful eye (lookout) and care (directions) of Babs, sparrows in the backyard by Genius-Gene alone in clever traps of his own invention, and crickets under the radiators and in dark corners of the house by all four members of the household and participants in the feast, each in the on-all-fours position.

In the middle of the night Eugen Winter heard Gene clambering up the stairs to his room, breathing heavily through his adenoidal nose as was his custom. He climbed under the covers into Eugen Winter's bed and the two slept like two babes in each other's arms until morning. (No hint at anything sexual here or on the numerous occasions in the future.)

7. comet

It is night. Eugen Winter walks in a crowd of people down the street. It is dark but the night is starry and he can see the outlines of the people around him, trees on the sides of the street, houses, and so on. Everyone is hurrying. Something urgent is driving them on.

Friendship also seems to unite the people. They have something in common and have to stick together. Eugen Winter doesn't see them but he knows that the Sommers—Phil, Babs, and Gene—are close by. In fact he knows that the first two are on his left and the third on his right. He searches with his right hand for Gene's, finds it, and takes it into his. It is soft and warm and makes him feel good. He keeps on walking.

They come out into an open area. It is overgrown with trees. It must be a park. They get in among the trees and keep on walking.

The walking gets laborious. They are climbing a hill. The climbing continues for a long time. The hill must be tall. People talk to each other to ease the burden of walking as they move along. Eugen Winter exchanges comments with Phil and Babs. He can hear Gene making noises on his right. He is no longer holding the latter's hand but feels safe and at ease as he does at home among them. Suddenly they all are out in the open. They have reached the top of the hill. It is empty of trees. People gather in a spot facing in one direction. There are quite a few of them—a few hundred at least, perhaps a thousand.

Lately there has been talk of a meteorite striking the earth in some distant future—thirty years or so. Apparently one has been spotted that might collide with the earth. There has been talk of governments getting together and formulating a plan for saving the earth. This would involve sending a probe to the meteorite and hitting it so as to set it off on a different path. The people have gathered here to do their share.

The landscape stretches flat before them to the horizon studded with lights in houses and streets. The sight is beautiful. The sky presents a similar picture above. There is no moon in it and it is studded with stars. The meteorite—a comet—is seen taking up about a third of the sky on the right. The head of the comet—the meteorite itself—is a shining bright spot and the tail a vast fan-like expanse of light. The comet resembles a peacock with a bright eye and an enormous spread tail.

The comet is speeding toward the earth and people will try deflecting it with their voices. They open their mouths, aim them at the comet, and give jointly one big mooing sound, Moooooo!

They repeat it again and again. The sound is powerful and unified as if made by one mouth. Eugen Winter feels wonderful about what is happening. He wants to go on mooing. He wants to be part of this crowd which is making the comet go away.

The comet seems to have shifted a little. It appears to be moving in a slightly different direction. With every mooing sound the people make it shift just a little more. They are making progress. They have to continue until the danger is gone.

8. cows

The sky was a huge round baby blue plate with the sun a giant egg yolk sliding around on it, first on one side, then way on the other. The landscape on both sides of the highway sparkled as if freshly washed or painted a brilliant green. In the first case it seemed to be made from green rubber and be ready to squeak when rubbed by fingers, in the second one the paint seemed not to have dried yet. Barns were maroon polyhedrons, silos—silver rectangles with one side semicircular, farm houses—white polyhedrons tending toward rectangles. The land was divided by the dotted lines of barbed wire fences into squares for future use whose nature had not yet been determined. The four-lane, divided concrete highway hummed softly under the wheels like a cat purring as it carried the car up and down gentle hills and along broad valleys.

They stopped off for a snack at a diner some hundred feet off the road and had toasted tuna fish salad and Swiss cheese sandwiches washed down with strawberry milkshakes.

Half an hour later they had to pull off the highway into an unpaved country lane surrounded by shady woods for Eugen Winter and Gene to relieve themselves. The two stood by the side of the road facing the woods and peed, each straining to reach the farthest across the wide ditch running along the side of the road. Gene watched Eugen Winter furiously out of the corner of his eye to imitate his impressive technique but wasn't able to master it and the latter won handily by nearly three feet. He had reached way into the woods, under a bush. Phil and Babs stayed in the car parked a couple of dozen feet back close to the highway discretely looking the other way.

As they drove on Eugen Winter kept peeking into the side roads they passed (mostly unpaved country lanes surrounded by woods) hoping to catch a glimpse of a schoolgirl on her way home from classes squatting down while peeing as he had seen sometimes on his visits to Germany as a child when it was a relatively common sight. But he didn't see any. These were country lanes, it was a weekend, he was in a different country, and most importantly times had changed. No one peed in the open any more.

After another couple of hours of driving they pulled off the highway and meandered along a country road paved with asphalt shiny and black as freshly mined coal that wound its way among steep hills perfectly round like giant mole hills overgrown with grass. They cast round shadows onto each other and onto the surrounding fields making the landscape a land of black polka dots on a bright green background.

Gene was growing more and more excited by the minute, fidgeting in his seat next to Eugen Winter, uttering muffled half-formed sounds and pointing with his fingers in this or that direction.

Suddenly he gave out a loud groan and then made a beautifully shaped mooing sound, deep and velvety as a note produced on a cello by a bow in the hand of an expert musician. His hand then shot up and pointed stiffly in the direction of a hill they were passing.

Eugen Winter looked toward where the hand ending in a sharp finger was aimed and saw on the profile of the hill above them the outline of three cows, still and solid, as if cast in bronze, looking intelligently at the car making its way along the road below.

They had almost arrived.

9. ok hamlet

The play is based on Shakespeare's *Hamlet*. The name was suggested by Gene Sommer's replying, OK Hamlet, that is, making simultaneous O and K signs with the fingers of one hand, which is his standard sign of approval, and saying, Huh-huh, huh-huh, in response to being presented with the story of *Hamlet* and the proposal for him to take part in its production.

cast of characters

Claudius: Phil Sommer

Hamlet: Gene Sommer

Polonius: Gerhardt, an old Guernsey ox

Horatio: Eugen Sommer (He changed his last name legally two weeks earlier.)

Gertrude: Babs Sommer

Ophelia: Gertrud, a young Guernsey cow

Ghost of Hamlet's father: Herbert, an old Hereford bull

Courtiers, ladies, officers, soldiers, etc.: various Angus, Guernsey, Hereford, and Holstein cows, oxen, heifers, and steers

The performance takes place at the Sommer family farm in the enclosure specifically put up for the occasion in front of the hay barn. The barn maroon, two stories high. The door of the barn wide open, with an area on the ground floor some twenty feet by twenty feet serving as the auditorium. The enclosure—mostly grass-covered ground some forty feet by forty feet surrounded on all sides except along the barn by a rail fence, with a gate in the far corner house left. The gate open. A long, single-storied likewise maroon building some fifty feet away from the gate house left, one of its doors open. It is the cow barn. A passageway surrounded by a rail fence leading from the gate to the door of the cow barn. A stubby silver silo in the distance sticking up from behind it.

The audience—eleven teenagers from the local school for alternatively intelligent children and two chaperone teachers seated on bales of hay or the straw-covered floor.

It is seven PM, a warm, sunny, early summer evening.

Claudius and Gertrude, the former near the far corner house left next to the gate, the latter in the far corner house right, seated on bales of hay. The heads of both bare. Gertrude's hair full of pink plastic curlers making it look like a crown. Both are dressed in old, white terry-cloth bath robes tied with belts. Claudius has a blue foam-rubber sword stuck under his belt and wears blue thongs on his bare feet. Gertrude's feet also bare with pink pom-pommed bathroom slippers on them.

From the cow barn emerges Horatio leading Hamlet by his hand. Horatio in a cowboy outfit—black hat, checkered blue and white shirt, Levi's supported by a wide belt with a big buckle, and light brown boots. Hamlet in a Tyrolean hat, white shirt, Lederhosen with a big orange foam-rubber sword stuck inside them, its tip sticking out below, white, tasseled knee-high socks, and heavy mountain-climber boots.

The two come to the middle of the enclosure and Horatio bows toward the audience followed by Hamlet. Claudius and Gertrude stand up, bow the same as Horatio and Hamlet, and sit down.

The audience applauds enthusiastically.

Hamlet sticks out his head toward the audience and moos. Horatio stops Hamlet quickly by putting his hand over the latter's mouth.

The audience applauds enthusiastically with some of its members mooing back. They are stopped by the chaperones.

With Hamlet quieted down Horatio runs to the cow barn and comes out leading Ghost of Hamlet's Father. They walk toward the gate, pass through it, and stop in the middle of the enclosure not far away from Hamlet. Horatio bows, followed by Hamlet.

The audience applauds enthusiastically with one or two of its members mooing but they are once again stopped by the chaperones.

Horatio motions for Hamlet to come. Hamlet comes up and puts his arms around Ghost of Hamlet's Father's neck. The latter stands still. Hamlet kisses the Ghost of Hamlet's Father on the neck and makes a long mooing sound.

The audience applauds enthusiastically with some of its members mooing. This time and from this point on for the rest of the performance the chaperones no longer make any attempts at preventing members of the audience from mooing.

Hamlet bows. Horatio leads Ghost of Hamlet's Father out of the enclosure back to the cow barn. After a minute he comes out leading Polonius. He leads the latter through the gate to the middle of the enclosure next to Hamlet. Hamlet tries to put his arms around the latter's neck and kiss him but is stopped by Horatio. Hamlet moos and bows to the audience.

The audience applauds enthusiastically with many of its members mooing.

Horatio motions for Hamlet to stab Polonius. Hamlet tries to pull out his sword, has some difficulty with it, then succeeds, and stabs Polonius in the belly and then other parts of the body. Polonius stoically ignores the attempts at hurting him and remains still. Hamlet goes on stabbing Polonius. Horatio stops him from doing it, slaps Polonius on the back, and the latter lies down obediently. Horatio slaps Polonius on the belly and the latter rolls over on his side. He lies there still. Horatio bows to the audience. Hamlet does the same and tries to stick the sword back inside his Lederhosen but has difficulty doing it. Horatio helps him out.

The audience applauds enthusiastically with some of its members mooing.

Horatio motions for Hamlet to stay behind and runs toward the cow barn. He comes out immediately leading Ophelia whose head is lavishly decorated with blue and white plastic flowers. He brings her to the middle of the enclosure, gives her a slap on the back, and she lies down obediently next to Polonius. Hamlet kneels down beside her, puts his arms around her neck, gives her a kiss on it, and then on the forehead. Ophelia indifferently ignores his professions of love and remains still.

Horatio slaps Polonius. The later stands up immediately. Ophelia does the same without being slapped. The two turn around on their own and walk toward the gate. Horatio follows them, they walk along the passageway, and disappear in the door. Hamlet moos after them.

The audience applauds enthusiastically with some of its members mooing.

Horatio comes out of the door carrying a cow's skull. He goes up to Hamlet and gives it to him. Hamlet raises the skull up with both hands and shows it to the audience as a bullfighter a trophy he has won. He parades with it around the enclosure strutting proudly as a bullfighter with a trophy in a bull ring.

The audience applauds enthusiastically.

Horatio tries to take the skull from Hamlet but the latter refuses. A tug of war ensues between the two.

The audience applauds enthusiastically with one member mooing briefly.

Gertrude gets up from her bale of hay, runs up to the two men struggling, relieves Horatio from his difficult task who looks grateful for her coming to his help, and takes the skull away from Hamlet. She censures him silently and he turns calm. Gertrude ignores him and walks back to her bale of hay, sits down, and puts the skull on the ground behind her.

Hamlet runs to get the skull back but Horatio stops him. He whispers something in Hamlet's ear and the latter turns calm. Horatio runs quickly to the cow barn and comes out leading Ghost of Hamlet's Father with one hand and carrying a pitcher full of water in the other. Passing by Claudius he hands him the pitcher and leads Ghost of Hamlet's Father to the middle of the enclosure. He then turns toward Claudius. Claudius gets up and joins him. Horatio slaps Ghost of Hamlet's Father on the back and the latter lies down. Horatio slaps Ghost of Hamlet's father again and the latter lies on his side. Claudius pours water in Ghost of Hamlet's Father's ear. Ghost of Hamlet's Father doesn't like it but stoically endures the trial. Hamlet runs up to Claudius, tears the pitcher out of Claudius' hand, and pours the rest of the water over Ghost of Hamlet's Father's head. This is too much for the latter, he shakes his head, quickly gets up, and runs on his own to the gate and then to the cow barn. Horatio runs after him. Claudius slaps Hamlet on the hand, tears the pitcher away from him, tells him by gestures to stay in place, walks back to his bale of hay, puts the pitcher on the ground behind it, and sits down. Hamlet moos toward the audience.

The audience applauds enthusiastically with all non-chaperone members mooing.

Horatio comes out of the door of the cow barn driving some twenty courtiers, etc. before him. Among them are Ghost of Hamlet's Father, Ophelia, and Polonius. They walk obediently through the gate and congregate in the middle of the enclosure. Claudius closes the gate. A sign of concern appears on Gertrude's face when he does this but she says nothing. The courtiers, etc. stand quiet, waiting for what is to come.

The audience applauds enthusiastically with many of its members mooing.

Hamlet moos back at them. Claudius, who is still by the gate, pulls the sword from under his belt and walks toward Hamlet. Hamlet's back is turned to him. Claudius nudges Hamlet with his sword. Hamlet turns around, sees Claudius has a sword in his hand, this time pulls his out easily, and lunges at Claudius. A sword fight ensues. Many of the members of the audience stand up, some of them getting up on their bales of hay to see better because the courtiers, etc. block their view of the fight. The fight continues for about a minute until Hamlet stabs Claudius in the chest and the latter falls face down on the ground. He lies with his arms stretched out, the sword still in his hand, pretending to be dead. Hamlet stabs him furiously a few times in the back and then looks up, not sure what to do. Finally he decides to stab a lady near him. He does this but Horatio stops him, turns him toward Gertrude, and gives him a push. Hamlet runs to Gertrude and stabs her in the stomach. She falls over onto the bale of hay on her back, her legs spread apart and arms hanging down, pretending to be dead. Hamlet stabs her furiously all over a few times, then turns around and looks at Horatio, not sure what to do. Horatio motions for him to stab other personages. Hamlet runs to the closest courtier, stabs him furiously, then stabs a young lady, then a young officer or soldier, and proceeds running through the enclosure stabbing everyone he comes across, emitting loud hair-raising sounds.

In the meantime Claudius has gotten up, walked back to his bale of hay, thrown the sword behind it, sat down, and is watching what Hamlet is doing with admiration. Gertrude has sat up too and does the same. Horatio has moved out of the way himself and stands next to the fence house left, in the middle, leaning on it, with one foot on the rail cowboy-fashion, likewise watching Hamlet going through his routine with admiration.

The audience applauds enthusiastically with some of its members emitting sounds similar to Hamlet's and other mooing.

Hamlet runs around the enclosure stabbing everyone he comes across and screaming wildly. The courtiers, etc. get excited and try to get away from Hamlet. The ones close to the hay barn explore the possibility of hiding there but are stopped by the chaperones. The non-chaperone members of the audience are frightened and scream wildly. Some cry out in fear. Many of them get up on top of the bales of hay they have been sitting on, others run deeper into the barn. The courtiers, etc. realize they cannot enter the barn and move in the other direction toward the gate. Those of the courtiers, etc. that have been close to the gate have congregated next to it already wanting to get out. Unable to do it they turn around and try moving the other way. There they find Hamlet stabbing them furiously. A pandemonium ensues. Courtiers, etc. moo, run around the enclosure, some of them dropping cow pies. Some of the courtiers, etc. slip on the latter. Hamlet does the same a few times, soiling his shoes, socks, and knees. He remains unstoppable however. Horatio and Claudius look on concerned with what is going on but not knowing what to do. Horatio has gotten up on the fence to get out of the way of the panicked courtiers, etc. and stands on the middle rail while holding on to the top one with his hands, his head turned left so as to see what is going on   Gertrude has been standing next to her bale of hay also looking at what is going on with concern. Finally she decides to act. She gestures furiously at Claudius to open the gate. He realizes immediately this is what should have been done long time ago and does as he is told. The courtiers, etc. near the gate see it is open, run to it, through it, down the passageway, and disappear in the door of the cow barn. Other courtiers, etc. notice what their companions have done and do the same. The enclosure starts emptying out. Hamlet pursues the stragglers. A little more and all the courtiers, etc. are gone. Hamlet runs down the passageway after the last one. Horatio runs after him, grabs him by his free hand, and brings him back to the enclosure. Gertrude grabs Hamlet's other hand, takes the sword out of it, holds onto it, takes Hamlet's hand in hers, and the three walk to the middle of the enclosure. Claudius follows them. Gertrude recalls Hamlet soiling himself on the cow pies and looks down at his legs. An expression of disgust appears on her face. She checks if Hamlet's hand she is holding is soiled and is pleased to find out that it isn't. She doesn't seem to worry about his other hand. (It is clean.) The four come to the middle of the enclosure, Claudius takes Gertrude's hand with the sword in it in his, they all bow toward the audience, and let go of each

other's hands on straightening up. Gertrude turns toward Hamlet
implying he is to do something. He remembers what it is, lifts his
right hand up, makes the intricate sign of "OK," and calls out,
Huh-huh, huh-huh, grinning from ear to ear.

The audience doesn't respond at first, apparently not
understanding Hamlet's gesture but then corrects itself, applauds
even more enthusiastically than on the other two occasions, most
of its members cheering and the rest mooing.

10. eugen sommer

A three-rail wooden fence with posts supporting it about ten feet
apart running left to right some thirty feet up ahead and an
identical fence perpendicular to the first one starting on its left
and going back, the end of the first fence on the right and of the
second one on the left not visible however. A stubby silver silo
sticking up in the distance on the extreme right of the first fence,
a long and low maroon building hugging the ground behind it.
Both the silo and the building flat-looking like props on a stage
rather than three-dimensional objects. The ground slopes gently
down toward the first fence. A narrow but relatively deep brook
in places not more than a foot wide running left to right some ten
feet behind the first fence its banks sloping down toward the
center and overgrown with thick short grass, giving it a vaguely

erotic appearance like that of a pudendum with tumid *labia majora* and hidden *labia minora* sheltering under pubic hair. Some hundred yards beyond the brook the land beginning to slope upward culminating in treeless rolling hills covered with short grass that stretch to the horizon. Their curving shapes likewise somewhat erotic like seductive female forms. It is winter but there is no snow on the ground. The land looks brown and soft as after recent heavy rains. The sky above it a uniform gray with no variegation in it as if from inherent grayness rather than being covered with clouds.

Eugen Sommer appears from somewhere in the back on the left and walks in a slow swaggering cowboy-style stride toward the first fence. He wears a black cowboy hat, a red and black checkered lumber jacket with a blue and white checkered shirt under it, Levi's, and light brown cowboy boots. In his left hand he caries a wooden sick about nine inches long and three quarters of an inch thick covered with gray bark one end of it whittled down to a pointed tip.

In spite of moving slowly he covers the ground surprisingly fast as in a movie and soon finds himself by the fence. He stops, rests his arms on the top rail, and stares ahead at the landscape before him. He does this for only a few seconds however and then gets up on the fence and sits down with his left hip and thigh on it

while supporting himself with his right foot on the middle rail.
He takes a big switchblade knife with a horn handle out of the
right pocket of his jacket, opens it by pressing the release button,
and proceeds whittling away at the sharpened end of the stick
while turning it from time to time in his fingers. The blade is
sharp and it cuts easily onto the soft wood shaving off big white
chunks of it which fall silently to the ground.

He watches this for a while and then lifts up his head, turns it left
together with his torso, and looks at the landscape as he had done
before. He continues whittling away at the stick however without
looking down at his hands as if sure the knife has mastered the
task assigned to it and will do it properly on its own. The knife in
fact does this, carrying out its task eagerly like someone with
limited intelligence delighting in having learned something and
being able to do it well. The shavings keep flaking off the stick
and fall to the ground one after another and the stick grows
shorter and shorter.

Eugen Sommer continues staring ahead. One would think there
is something particular in the landscape that attracts his attention
but this apparently isn't so. He isn't focusing on anything but
gazes vacantly into the distance. It is possible he isn't even aware
there is anything there. His eyes must be irritated somewhat
because moisture keeps welling up in them and he has to blink

from time to time to get rid of it. It gathers in the corners of his eyes then and stays there for a while before evaporating. There is never enough of it to form a tear however.

years of travel

I. the mirror

It was late morning. Franz stood in front of the mirror on the
wall above the dresser in his bedroom shaving. The mirror was
rectangular with a brown wooden frame and he saw himself in it—
his thick black hair shiny with water combed back and parted in
the middle, thick black eyebrows, pale blue eyes, straight long
nose with a bump in the middle, ruddy complexion above the
thick snow-like lather covering his cheeks and the lower part of his
face, white shirt unbuttoned at the top with the low collar to
which he would later attach the high starched one, gray
suspenders running over his shoulders and continuing parallel
down the sides of his chest where they joined his pants. He
couldn't see the latter but had a clear image of them as if they
were in front of his eyes—tight-fitting and black, made from shiny
serge material. Black low-heeled boots with pointed toes and
elastic on the sides protruded from under them. He visualized
these less clearly as if they were hidden in a layer of fog that
covered the floor. His right hand with its little finger sticking out
attached to the thick hairy forearm that protruded out of the
rolled-back sleeve moved up and down next to his face holding
the razor by its yellow bone handle. The left one made the task
easier by pulling with its fingers on the skin on the face and neck

in the proper places. Way in the back could be seen the wallpaper on the opposite wall—gray flowery pattern similar to clouds in the sky on a blue background.

As the lather collected on the blade Franz would wipe the latter off on a small white linen towel that lay on the right side next to the white enameled basin half-filled with soapy water. The white soap mug with his name "Franz" in black Gothic letters and with the brush in it stood on the other side of the basin. His beard was thick and the razor made a crackling noise as it moved down the skin like a bratwurst busily frying in a skillet.

It was quiet in the apartment except for the crackling made by the razor and then his wife's voice was heard coming from the adjoining parlor. It was unclear and nasal as if muffled by a big wad of cotton.

Franz's wife: The clock has stopped again.

Franz (*continuing to shave throughout the conversation, annoyed*): Wind it.

Franz's wife: I can't. The gear is stuck.

Franz: Pull hard on the chain.

Franz's wife (*annoyed herself*): I did!

Franz: Pull on the right weight first and then immediately on the left one... while you're pulling on the right. The mechanism is broken. I told you.

An indistinct peeved sound is heard from his wife followed by a mechanical clicking sound like that of teeth chattering very fast and evenly. Then silence.

Franz (*after waiting a while*): Did it work?

No answer.

Franz (*after waiting about that long again, somewhat louder*): Gretel, did it work?

Franz's wife (*reluctantly*): Yes.

Franz: See, I told you before.... You keep forgetting.

Franz's wife (*peeved*): It keeps getting stuck!

Franz made a deep sigh. He wanted to say something but stopped himself, knowing from experience this wouldn't lead to anything positive. He had finished shaving his cheeks and was now working on his chin. The newly exposed skin shone red as if from cold.

The mirror reverses everything, mused Franz—left is right and right is left. But why doesn't it reverse the other way—top—bottom and bottom—top? Is it the way the mirror is made? If he were to rotate it so that the vertical side became the horizontal one on top, would his feet show up on top in it? No, of course not. It doesn't and it would 't make sense. Mirrors are rotated all the time and nothing of the sort happens.

His puzzlement persisted however.

If he were to tilt his head ninety degrees to the left, would his chin show up on the left and the top of his head on the right? He thought that would be crazy, in other words that that of course wouldn't happen, but still he did tilt his head left as far as he comfortably could and saw no difference as he expected.

What in hell is going on here? He wondered. There must be something in the property of the glass then that makes this happen.... No the glass couldn't have anything to do with it because if you rotated the mirror it made no difference.

Was it gravity then? Did the force of gravity make the mirror behave in such a way that it reversed things one way and didn't the other?

That also sounded absurd. He stopped shaving and pondered. Staring back at him was his face with the right ear and eye being the left ones and the left ones the right ones. But the right ones in the mirror were the real left ones and the other way around. So the mirror didn't reverse the physical things but just the names, what the physical things were called—right—left and left—right. But that too was amazing, even more so if you think about it than if it were to reverse physical things. To reverse the meaning of words, something invisible, is really something!

He stood staring at himself in the mirror, chills running up his spine and the hair on his head stirring, unable to breathe. It was scary the way the world was made.

2. train ride

The train cheerfully chugged along through the flat rural landscape, the little black coal-burning engine trailing a giant plume of gray smoke showing off what it could do and that it could do more, the three short stubby cars their top halves dark green, nearly black, metal, the lower ones—yellow varnished wood, behind it, having no other choice but to follow, jerkily bobbing up and down like corks in water, swinging from one side of the tracks to the other threatening to come off, the fields of rye, wheat, corn, beets, potatoes, etc., or just grass, a shiny solid green as if freshly painted or just taken out of and still dripping with water, the also freshly ironed pale blue percale sky stretched tight without a wrinkle above them.

Franz sat in the corner on the comfortably molded wooden bench of the same wood as the lower half of the cars on the outside, his right shoulder pressed against the wall, facing in the direction of the movement of the train, his hair, face, and vision deformed by the air rushing in through the open window mixed with the smoke coming from the engine that smelled of hard-boiled eggs and the memories the latter brought with it. The few passengers scattered along the benches in the car stayed invisible, lost in the emptiness as among mirrors.

The engineer, Franz knew, stood leaning out the side of the engine his round face also distorted by the air rushing by, munching on a big wedge of dark bread cut out of a huge loaf and a peeled onion white and almost as big as his face, from time to time checking his big silver watch similar to his face and even more to the onion which he would pull out of his vest from under the gray canvas engineer's jacket soiled with coal dust.

The landscape made loud squeaking noises as the train moved through it like a rubber duck played with under water.

At times the train would pass stations it didn't have to stop at, trim single-storied rectangular structures with tiled roofs, the luxuriant nasturtiums in the flower pots hung off their wide eaves looking like pots of burning kerosene fanned by the draft. The platforms in front of them were paved with tiles shiny and neat like bars of chocolate stripped bare of tin foil. Toy station masters made from lead and painted garish colors stood still with their feet together, arms permanently joined to their bodies, holding in the right one bent at the elbow a sign with a red circle on a white background on the end of a short stick.

It was still early in the day but people—typical of workers' families—were already having their simple suppers—mashed potatoes and buttermilk, cottage cheese mixed with sour cream, radishes, and scallions eaten with dark bread, scrambled eggs prepared on the handy portable *Primus* kerosene stoves. The buildings were so close to the tracks that Franz could feel his cheek brush past those of some of the people at the tables even through the pressure of the wind.

The sun was invisible yet obviously there, but then suddenly like a big new shiny coin slipping out of the pocket and burying itself between the cushions in a sofa it slid down, stuck behind the horizon, and it was night.

3. the rectory

The sharp black iron bars of the fence couldn't hold back the riot of colors in the flower beds behind them which nonetheless eventually turned proper, dutifully taking on rectangular and rounded forms, and the soft darkness in the open windows in the stone facade of the house was so inviting that Franz's sudden desire to be there was physically painful like a stab with a long needle that penetrated way into his chest.

Why not knock on the door and ask to see the priest? He thought. Priests are expected to be available to anyone needing to speak to them about vital things, so why should this one refuse him? This is what he would do, he decided and with a feeling of joy like a vast breathtaking vista opening up before him he stopped, turned right, walked up to the gate in the fence, and put his hand on it. Such an impulsive act was very much out of character with him and he was experiencing something that was completely novel. He realized he had always envied people who were able to behave spontaneously and now finally he was doing it himself. How wonderful!

The gate opened with a gentle tinkling sound—a bell disturbed by his movement. He hadn't noticed it was there. It was like the ringing you hear in a church during the communion and it seemed to be specifically designed to welcome him into his new way of living. He had done the right thing! He closed the gate behind him and found himself in the garden.

The esthetically curving stone path led him to the sturdy varnished arched oak door in the stone facade. He brought his hand to the bronze knocker in the shape of a clenched fist and knocked with it three times.

The sound it made could be heard traveling through the house but then it died down and silence followed it. Was there no one inside? He wondered, disappointment rising up in him. It looked as though he was not to free himself from his shell of propriety after all.

Then however faint noises started coming from the depth of the house like those made by mice rummaging and chewing on something inside walls and finally footsteps could be heard nearing the door gradually getting louder and louder. No, his life was going to be different from this moment on after all.

The door was opened by a slender young woman with a very pale complexion and thin blond hair tied in the back—so light it was barely distinguishable from her skin. Her pale blue eyes were almost the same color as her skin and hair so that her head seemed a pale stain. The woman—girl, really—wore a plain dress of thin fabric in a flowery pattern, the flowers almost as pale as the rest of her. Franz felt as if what was before him was the absence of the girl rather than her herself.

Yes, the girl said, could she help him?

A little flustered since he expected to be facing a man—the priest—Franz hesitated but then got a hold of himself and asked if he could see the priest.

Father Koch? The girl asked.

Yes, Franz replied after another brief hesitation since he didn't know the priest's name and momentarily wondered if perchance there was more than one priest living there which was possible. It didn't matter however, so his saying yes was alright.

Father Koch was out momentarily, the girl answered. (There appeared to be only one priest living there after all.) But he would be back soon. Would he, Franz, like to come in and wait for him?

Yes he would, Franz replied readily and full of enthusiasm stepped into the house as the girl moved aside to let him pass.

She would take him into the living room, she said, shut the door, moved past him, and led him down the short hallway to the room on the left through the already open door. He obediently followed her and stepped over the threshold.

He had his breath almost literally knocked out of him when he did that. Sunshine so strong it seemed a physical force was bursting into the room through an open window in the wall opposite the door blinding him completely. It felt like a powerful blow delivered to his midriff. Paralyzed he stood still unable to move.

Would he please sit down, the girl said pointing to a chair at the near right edge of the table which ran practically the length of the room from one end to the other down its middle with chairs, perhaps a dozen of them, around it. A cabinet along the wall on the left and a sideboard along the one on the right comprised the rest of the furniture. It appeared to be a dining room rather than a living room although apparently it was used for both eating in and lounging. Franz seemed to be able to see only because of the shadow the girl's hand cast on the objects shielding them from the sun.

Franz sat down in the chair and closed his eyes. Everything was black anyway after the blinding window and he might as well let his eyes came back to normal under his eyelids.

In the darkness he heard the girl excuse herself and promise she would be right back. He didn't hear her footsteps but when he opened his eyes she was gone.

Silence reigned in the house and he wondered what the girl was doing. He had turned sideways so as not to be blinded by the sun but in the end was unable to hold himself back from glancing at the window again fascinated by its brightness. He shielded his eyes with his hand but to his surprise saw that it wasn't as bright as before. Had the sun moved that far in the little time that had passed since he had looked at it the first time? Not likely. The chair was merely in a different spot from where he had stood before and was now sitting down.

The brief moment was dragging on and on and Franz's curiosity about what lay outside the window permitting the sun to shine so bright through it got the better of him and he got up and gingerly walked up to it keeping his hand ready to shield his eyes when he would have to.

When he stood by the window the sun didn't blind him although he could feel its heat on his face. He nearly fell over for a second time when he looked out however—right under the window there was a huge pit some thirty or forty feet deep. Its banks were steep but not to the degree that you couldn't climb up and down them if you were careful.

The pit was shaped like a truncated cone and on the bottom of it there was a flat area some ten feet in diameter with water gathered in it in puddles as well as big triangular pieces of glass. The water and the glass reflected strong white light and it seemed it was coming from inside the earth as if another world lay beneath it airy and bright. For an instant Franz thought it was this light that had blinded him but dismissed the thought immediately. He could feel the hot sunlight on his face prickling it like blood hardening on his skin. The other light was different.

Four or five Orthodox Jewish boys between twelve and fourteen years of age were milling about in the flat area bent down, eyes fixed on the ground, looking for something. They were dressed in caftans and tight britches fastened below the knees, both made from a shiny black material, their legs in white stockings and feet in slippers open at the end. On their heads they wore black skullcaps from the same material as the caftans and britches over closely cropped hair. Long luxurious side locks swayed gracefully along the sides of their faces as they moved around gracefully as if to the sound of sweet music.

What in God's name are they looking for and why is the pit right under the window? Franz wondered but at that instant heard the girl's voice behind his back on the left saying she was sorry for having left him alone for so long.

Franz jerked with surprise and then blushed and turned hot all over at what he felt was an uncalled for temerity with which he had behaved in a house he had forced his way into. He should have waited patiently in his chair. He mumbled something to the effect that he wanted to see what it was like outside the window and with his head bent down in shame walked back to his chair and sat down on it. The girl ignored his words as if not having heard them.

When he raised his head he saw she was sitting at the other end of the table diagonally across from him her chair pushed away.

Bright but cold flashes of light burst forth at regular intervals from her hands which moved quickly and constantly at the level of her midriff accompanied by dry metallic sounds. Because the chair was pushed away from the table he could see a big ball of pink yarn sitting comfortably in her lap and a long flat and also pink item that had draped itself like a cat over her knees. She was knitting and had clearly stepped out of the room earlier to pick up what she was working on.

4. the pit

The girl stays silent with her head bent down, looking closely at the needles as if fascinated by their motions, unable to tear her eyes away, seemingly oblivious of him. Her bringing her knitting seems to imply they would wait for the priest for a long time. "Back soon" must have been just a socially motivated euphemism. And they apparently would sit like this in silence until the man came. It might take hours! Franz scolds himself for having given in to his crazy whim but at that instant the girl speaks up.

The girl (*without lifting her eyes from the knitting, casually, as if to herself*): You doubt if you have an immortal soul?

Franz (*startled, almost jumping up as if from a loud noise next to his ear, then realizes what the question means, is confused, and does not know how to answer):* Me?... Doubt?... *(The issue has not been a burning one with him although he has pondered it on a few occasions without having resolved it. Thinks of saying" yes" but feels that would sound too definite. Decides on "no.")* No. *(It doesn't come out too convincing however.)*

The girl *(as if not having heard him, clearly having made up her mind beforehand):* It's natural to have doubts. Most people do. All have them at one time or another in their lives.

Franz *(realizes the girl thinks he is ashamed to admit having doubts and rebels against it):* But I don't!

The girl *(interrupting him, thinks he is ashamed after all):* People come to father Koch all the time... at least once a week... mostly young men like you. They're ashamed to admit it but they all want to be convinced that they have souls... immortal souls.

Franz feels angry, opens his mouth to interrupt her but suddenly decides not to do it. It doesn't matter. He relaxes and listened to the girl with interest. Is glad he has done it.

The girl *(continuing as before, watching the knitting needles do their incredible abstract dance in the air above her lap):* And he convinces them in the end. Maybe not at once... the first time... but they come a couple of more times and he convinces them... proves to them they have immortal souls... and they are peaceful... happy. They don't come any more. *(Changes the tone of her voice, feeling she has passed the first stage. Glances for an instant up and then lowers her eyes again. Doesn't look at Franz however.)* How can man not have a soul? You look at a piece of wood... a chopping block... and at a man. Do they look the same? No! Can a chopping block have a soul? No, it's just a piece of dead wood! Then a man must have a soul if he is different from a chopping block since he's alive. And since the soul is invisible... since it isn't wood, or stone, or flesh, then how can it die?

Franz feels even more relaxed than when the girl started talking. There is something convincing in her childish logic. Wants to close his eyes and listen to her. Feels glad as she goes on.

The girl *(after a pause, having organized her thoughts)*: Now an animal... a dog or a rooster... is different. They don't worry about whether or not they have souls. Did you ever see a dog or a rooster walk around sad, with its head down, not knowing what to do? *(She laughs and glances up at Franz. He smiles back at her and the smile continues on his face for a while like an oil slick on the surface of water.)* That's because they can't even think of having a soul... don't know what a soul means. And man does and it means that he has a soul.... For how could you wonder if you have a soul if you didn't have one? Has anyone seen it in someone else? No, they feel it in themselves.

The girl stops satisfied with herself and goes on knitting. Franz watches her with amazement. It has never occurred to him anyone like she could exist and think the way she does.

Time goes on. Eventually the sun is no longer in the window. Fresh air streams in through it together with occasional tattered sounds of voices. Franz thinks it must be the boys in the pit. They are still there. How strange the whole thing is. What is the purpose of the pit and what are the boys doing in it? The girl is totally absorbed in her knitting. All you can hear is the metallic clicking of the needles. Will he have to sit like this until the priest comes? And god knows when that will happen.

He watches the pink shape grow on the girls lap like a giant fetus. Is she pregnant?... By the priest?... Is she making a garment for the baby?... Unexpectedly, under internal pressure, he speaks up.

Franz: Is that a baby's garment you're knitting?... Are you going to have a baby?

The girl (*lifting up her face and looking at him with a kind smile*): It is a baby's garment... for my sister's baby. (*Adding in the same kind voice with the smile persisting on her face.)* I can't have babies. I have anemia. *(Smiles even wider.)* I'm not even married. *(Looks down again.)*

Franz keeps silent embarrassed by what he has uncovered with his question. Is surprised anemia would prevent a woman from having babies. Thinks it must be a particularly severe case. Wants to ask the girl about it but feels it would be inappropriate. Then realizes a perfectly good question has formed itself in his mind and that he has a right to know the answer to it.

Franz: Is the baby due soon?

The girl *(without raising her eyes)*: In about two months. *(Volunteers the extra information. It is clearly a topic dear to her heart.)* I will go to stay with my sister for a couple of months after that... to help her. It'll be tough for her alone. Her husband works and our mother is no longer with us.

Franz feels sad at the last bit of information. Also embarrassed he has uncovered it. He then realizes another perfectly reasonable question has formed itself in his mind and sees no reason why he shouldn't try getting an answer to it.

Franz: How is father Koch going to manage by himself? Will he get another housekeeper?

The girl (*raises her eyes for an instant and then lowers them again*): He won't need a live-in one... just someone to come and clean up once a week. The cooking he can do himself. He likes to do it when he can.... Says he would have been a cook if he hadn't become a priest. I cook just everyday meals.... He cooks for special occasions.

Franz listens with interest to what the girl says. Waits for her to continue when she stops.

The girl (*after a few seconds, as if on cue*): He says it's because of his name. (*Lifts up her face and looking at Franz laughs. She is referring to the fact that "Koch" means "cook" in German.*) He says if his last name were "Schuster" he would have liked making shoes. (*She is referring to the fact "Schuster" means "shoe maker" in German.*)

Franz laughs a hearty laugh.

The girl (*continuing in a normal voice, her mirth gone, the topic drawing more information out of her*): In fact that's what he's doing now. He's at the soup kitchen... helping out.

Franz (*startled and worried; thinks it might be hours before the priest comes home*): Oh....

The girl (*continuing to volunteer*): They're having tripe... his favorite dish. He fixes it real well... his own recipe... from his mother... with vinegar. It's delicious.

Franz's taste buds wake up. He notices saliva has collected in his mouth.

The girl (*after a brief pause*): He'll bring some home. (*Changes the tone of her voice.*) Do you like tripe?

Franz (*he does—his mother used to fix it deliciously too; enthusiastically*): Yes.

The girl (*almost as enthusiastically*): Why don't you have some with us? Father Koch will bring a lot of it... a whole bucket. He's very good-hearted. He'll be glad if you stay.

Franz (*hesitant but thrilled*): Alright.

The girl (*unable to stop showing her enthusiasm for the priest*): He's from Styria. That's where the recipe for the tripe's from. Speaks in a heavy accent. You might have trouble understanding it.

Franz is unable to say anything, simply smiles, and closes his eyes like a cat melting with pleasure—what a wonderful decisions he has made!

He realizes he cannot hear the boys' voices coming in through the window any more and wonders if they have gone away—climbed up the steep sides of the pit. Once again he is puzzled by the pit and them in it. He realizes then that he could resolve the issue very simply—he could ask the girl. They have gotten intimate enough for him to do that and he is sure she will tell him what is going on.

But then to his surprise he feels his curiosity has gone away like a balloon slowly going flat. He knows what the girl would answer him and knows the answer himself. The pit is there because it is needed in that spot and the boys are in it because they want to find something there. It is so simple. Why hadn't he figured it out before?

5. saints

It is night, dark. Franz seems to be in a farmyard. There are big buildings with small windows and tall wide doors all around and all sorts of farm machinery and vehicles here and there among them—combines, carts, plows, harrows, barrows. Straight ahead you can see outlines of trees—an orchard.

Franz is excited by the idea of being in among trees and walks on toward them. Soon he is there.

At first the orchard appears to be empty but then he hears strange noises coming from all directions and notices weird rounded shapes stirring on the ground.

His eyes have gotten used to the darkness and he can see better. He realizes these are people kneeling down bent over doing something with their hands. He looks closer and sees the people— all men—are digging with their fingers in the soil, pulling something out, putting it in their mouths, and chewing on it. They get the things while bending over and chew on them after they straighten up. They remain standing on their knees.

He realizes what is happening—these are saints who dig up worms from the soil and eat them. This is what saints do. It is part of being a saint.

He feels he wants to do the same. He has it in him to be a saint.

He finds a spot a few steps ahead which he feels is right for digging, kneels down, and digs his fingers into the ground.

The spot he has chosen is good. The soil in it is soft as if freshly plowed and his fingers penetrate into it with ease. He searches with them in it and soon feels something wet and cold wiggling around. It is a worm. He grabs it, pulls it out, straightens up, puts it in his mouth, and bites on it with his teeth. It wiggles desperately at first but his teeth break it up into pieces, then into smaller ones, and ultimately into a gooey paste which he pushes with the help of his tongue into his gullet and swallows.

It doesn't taste bad. It is insipid like beefsteak tartar without any seasoning and he is pleased with having made the choice. Being a saint isn't hard. He bends down again, digs in the soil, finds another worm, and eats it as the first one.

He does this a few more times but then unexpectedly feels nauseous. It isn't that the taste of worms has suddenly changed but that he finds the idea of eating them revolting. It is as if he didn't understand its meaning before but now he does.

He shudders at the thought of what he has been doing. His mouth fills with saliva, he bends over, sticks his head far out so as not to soil his clothes, spits the saliva out, retches a few times, and vomits. He vomits again and again and when he finishes he straightens up and looks around. His eyes have filled with tears and the world swims in them broken up into rounded forms. He hears strange noises again all around but now they are different than before. He looks closer and realizes that the other men in the garden—the saints—from time to time do the same as he has done—they interrupt their digging and chewing, retch, and vomit. Then they rest a while standing up on their knees before returning to what they had been doing. He will have to do the same.

He still feels nauseous and therefore has a right to rest and so he turns his head around and notices that it has gotten lighter. Instinctively he looks up and sees high up in the cloudless sky the moon white and huge but deformed as if suffering from elephantiasis.

The sight is frightening and he quickly turns his eyes away and looks at the ground.

Some ten or so yards up ahead he sees a narrow wooden structure—an outhouse. Suddenly a small gray creature crawls out from under it and then another one. These are rats. They stay close to where they have come out from and sniff the air checking if it is safe for them to proceed. The way seems to be clear for in a few seconds they take off and are gone. Then another rat comes running from somewhere and disappears under the side of the outhouse. The spot is different from the one the other two rats had come out from. It appears a bunch of rats live under the outhouse probably feeding on the contents of the cesspool.

Franz finds the idea revolting and shifts his eyes away once more. For the first time he notices the trees are all leafless. It is late fall. In the distance beyond the trees he sees a big building with many windows. It is the farmhouse. The windows are all dark and the house seems to bulge with darkness like an overstuffed package tied up with a twine. Then he hears a noise like giant millstones grinding away in the distance. It is the wind. He feels cold and instinctively hunches up his shoulders.

6. the rope

On the other side of the tracks the earth bulged in a little cramp of a hillock and three slender birch trees had staked their claim to it having strayed off some ten yards away from the crowded copse behind them. They dripped wet yellow leaves like candles hot wax burning too exuberantly.

The left pair of tracks strained to merge themselves with those on the right like curves becoming asymptotes to straight lines by definition intersecting with them at infinity. You couldn't see them do it because they disappeared in the thick morning fog long before that.

Beginning and end? The man asked. These are concepts the human mind has come up with and they aren't necessarily universal. Take a line for instance. It does have a beginning and an end—one on one side and the other one on the other. That is because it is open. But consider a circle. Where does it start and end? Nowhere. Does he agree?

He does, said Franz.

A circle is a closed line and has no beginning and no end, the man continued. The same is true of the surface of a sphere. It doesn't start nor end anywhere. It is a closed plane.

So does he then think that time has no beginning and no end? Franz asked. That it is like a circle or a sphere?

That is a possibility although we don't know if it is true, the man replied. There may be other alternatives which we cannot conceive.

Infinity? Franz asked looking at the tracks. That time is infinite? Without beginning or end?

No, he didn't have that in mind, the man replied. Something completely different which we are not even able to think of. But the concept of infinity is interesting however. Has he ever tried to envision it?

Yes he has, Franz answered eagerly. And he can't do it. How can you have something that goes on forever?

Precisely, the man said. The concept of infinity probably hints at the limitation of the human mind—faced with a situation which it can't comprehend, it comes up with an idea that has no instance in reality but which merely states that it has run into a problem it can't solve. Infinity of time and space probably don't exist but something completely different which we will never grasp.

And also beginning and end? Franz asked quickly.

Beginning and end of time and space, that is their limits? Yes, the man said. They are related to infinity. Infinity comes up when we try to imagine a world without beginning and end of both time and space.

And creation too? Franz went on. When the world was created?

Exactly, the man replied. This might mean that the world was never created and will never end and yet it isn't infinite at the same time.

It is bizarre, said Franz. And he can't comprehend it.

Neither can he, said the man. It is funny in a way because it contradicts all the rules according to which we live. And another principle which is suspect but which is related to beginning and end, that is which might not be universal but is inherent to the human mind, is the relationship of cause and effect. Can he imagine something happening without there being a cause for it? A chair for instance appearing in the middle of the room without anyone putting it there?

No, of course he can't, Franz replied smiling.

Neither can he nor any other human being, the man continued. But it doesn't mean that this is a universal relationship, that every event, that is effect, must have a cause, for instance the world itself. This is really where all the theories about the nature of the world run into difficulties. If everything has a cause then the world must have one too which means that it has been created.

And if it has been created then it must have a creator. But if it has a creator then what is the cause of the creator, or the cause of the cause? Does he see what the problem is? Reasoning like this has no end. So the concept of cause and effect cannot be universal. There must be some effect which has no cause and whether it is the world or its creator makes no difference. But what do you buy if you postpone the suppression of the relationship one stage? Nothing.

Yes, he agrees, said Franz.

So the most plausible explanation is that the world wasn't caused by an event meaning that it wasn't created, the man said. And yet we can't say either that it has always existed. The situation is most likely something else yet we will never be able to grasp it because our mind is incapable of doing it.

He leaned with his left elbow on his knee and the trumpet he clutched in his hand shone bright like a ray of sunshine he had managed to snatch out of the ashen morning light and shaped into a beautiful loop. Gray stubble covered his cheeks like sand as if he had been tossing around on the ground all night long unable to sleep.

Tossing around all night long unable to sleep searching for answers to life's persistent questions which have been gnawing on humanity's mind since its beginnings out of a profound love for it, thought Franz.

He must be Jewish with that melancholy face of his and the Talmudic wisdom, he continued, the love for humanity a result of the sensitivity to pain brought on by the countless injustices his people have endured through generations. Some cobbler too who moonshines as a musician at country dances, weddings, and christenings... and an occasional bar-mitzvah too for sure.

But why is the world the way it is? So crazy and complex? He blurted out unexpectedly to himself sensing with a pounding heart the nearness of the hoped-for revelation.

The answer is clear after all that has just been said, isn't it? Asked the man. It is the way it is because such is at least one of the possibilities for its being. If there are other possibilities then they too will take place or have taken place already. Has he ever had to unravel a long piece of rope that has being yanked around for a while?

Yes, he has, Franz once again said eagerly, understanding what was coming.

It tends to tie itself into the craziest knots, doesn't it? The man went on.

It sure does, said Franz suppressing the laughter rising up in his throat. And it is funny to think sometimes that it has done it by itself. You think that someone has done it on purpose.

Exactly! Said the man. And it is only a rope, a flexible line some twenty or thirty feet long, and it has been jerked around for a few minutes. Imagine what unbelievably crazy knots will result when you have such complex structures as atoms and molecules being shaken around for billions of years. Is it strange then that the world is the way it is?

The wisdom in the man's eyes shone like tears of compassion.

7. out of franz's diary

Yesterday, as I was sweeping, running with my usual animal-like seriousness the stiff brush over the dusty concrete floor and counting the little blue-black tacks like golden stars in a dark night sky, I realized dead silence reigned overt the shop like a wild scream. Frightened, I stopped, looked up, and saw in the opening leading to the next room a weird and ghastly figure—short, squat, dumpy, carrying something unbelievably strange in its left hand that reached almost to the ground. It was shapeless and ragged at the end, yellowish in color and translucent but with dark streaks in it here and there, in all resembling a splash of vomit flying out of the mouth of a drunken man. The figure—I realized it was a woman—had an empty, expressionless face and vague, unfocused eyes. Her mouth was partly open, as if her jaw were too weak to stay closed, and a barely audible sound was coming out of it like hissing from a poorly closed thermos bottle—a thin, monotonous wail. She was walking in short unsteady steps like a wardrobe waddling along while tilting from side to side, clearly aimlessly, her goal being merely to move rather than to get someplace. There was something unbelievably frightening about the woman, and after a few seconds I realized it was first of all because she wasn't carrying the strange object in her hand but by her elbow joint as if it were capable of holding something like a hand. Where her hand and forearm were wasn't clear.

It was one of the Slavic women who work in the pressing department, Ruthenian, I think, who, as I found out later, got her forearm crushed in the machine in which the skins are pressed after being sprayed. She had put in a skin inside the machine, it got wrinkled, she tried to smooth it out, when the woman on the other side, who operated the press, mistakenly hit the lever. The guard that was supposed to stop the press from coming down malfunctioned and the woman's forearm got caught inside and was squashed to the thinness of an animal's skin.

It was late afternoon, almost closing time, and sunlight was streaming into the shop through the window on the left which I could see with the corner of my eye, coloring the dirt-caked pane yellow, the same shade as the hideous shape dangling on the end of the woman's arm. By then I had realized what had happened, without knowing the details, and as I saw the connection between these two images, an overwhelming feeling of revelation came over me, as if I had received some important and happy news. It was like the joy you feel on a beautiful spring morning as you step out of the house after a good night's sleep. It was the truth I had been waiting for all my life and it came to me in that cramped, stuffy tannery, only days after I had taken that menial job with the hope of finding it, whereas I had looked for it in vain for years in the vast sumptuous spaces of Gothic and Baroque cathedrals.

8. the cello

Wan of face and bleary of eye from being up till dawn, mind hazy with alcohol and lack of sleep like a room with cigarette smoke, Franz stumbled his way through the empty forest its high-topped pine trees like pillars in a Gothic cathedral spaced deliberately in a random pattern for organic botanical effect toward the wall of white light at the end where he knew lay the sea.

It was empty too, gray and flat in spite of a strong wind blowing from its direction, intersecting on the horizon with the likewise gray and flat low sky. A strip of dull gray sand some thirty feet wide separated it from the strip of bright green grass half that width which ran along the edge of the wood. A slender figure on the edge of the water about a dozen feet to the right of him was the only vertical shape breaking up the horizontal monotony.

Franz stopped where the sand began. The figure was a girl, judging by the narrowness of her hips not more than fourteen. She stood with her back to the sea and the wind blew her loose blond hair and long dark dress landwards. Her face was dark against the bright background.

Seeing Franz she turned toward him and smiled, her white teeth illuminating for an instant her face like a match bursting out in a flame. Franz saw then that her eyes were unusually pale, luminous gray, with the eyelashes spreading out in all directions like the petals of a daisy.

He felt himself grow sober in an instant as if injected with a miraculous substance capable of neutralizing in a flash the alcohol in the blood.

The following scene then played itself out between him and the girl.

Franz (*moving toward the girl, smiling*): Good morning!

The girl (*smiling back*): Good morning!

Franz comes up to the girl, notices a dark shape lying on the sand on her right and a little to the back. Realizes it looks like a musical instrument. Thinks it must be a cello. Assumes it belongs to the girl. Is intrigued by this.

Franz (*excited*): Is that your cello? Did you spend the whole night on the beach playing it?

The girl (*laughing heartily*): No! I'm not a musician. I don't play any instrument. And I didn't spend the whole night on the beach. It's too cold... and dangerous. I just came out. The beach is beautiful in the morning... when there's no one around... all empty. (*Turns her head right and looks down at the instrument.*) It's

not a cello. It's a bass... very big.... The sea threw it out.
Someone must have thrown it away.

Franz is intrigued by the girl's words. He moves to the left, turns
right a little, squats down, and begins examining the instrument,
running his fingers over it. He sees to his surprise that most of it is
buried in the sand with only its lower left side sticking out. The
girl watches him while continuing to stand up.

Franz (*trying to move the instrument out of the sand and being unable to
do it*): It's buried in pretty deep.

He runs his fingers over the edge of the visible part of the
instrument and reconstructs in his mind its whole shape.
Remembers what the girl has said about it.

Franz: It's not a bass. It's a cello. (*Ponders.*) It looks big.... Maybe
it was especially made for a very big man.... But it's not a bass for
sure. (*After a pause.*) Maybe it just looks big because you don't see
all of it.... (*Tries to move the instrument again and once more is unable
to do it. Looks inside through the cut in its surface. Sees sand inside it.*)
It's full of sand. (*Pushes his fingers under it and tries to lift it up. Is
unable to do it.*) Heavy. (*Realizes the girl is still standing up. Has an
idea. Speaks while straining*) Maybe you could help me....

The girl moves over next to him. Squats down. Pushes her fingers into the sand under the edge of the instrument. Tries to lift it up with him. It still doesn't budge.

The girl (*giving up*): You can't do it. (*Stands up.*) I tried doing it myself but it's in too deep.

Franz once more runs his fingers along the edge of the visible part of the instrument. Moves them where the sand covers it on top. Digs his fingers in. Feels something sharp. Decides it is splinters. Concludes the instrument is broken there.

Franz: It's broken.... There's a hole in it. (*Ponders and tires to imagine how the instrument fits under the sand.*) I'm not sure it's all there. (*Ponders some more.*) The neck must be missing for sure... and probably most of the top.... (*Decides to investigate. Digs with his fingers in the sand.*) Let's see.

The girl (*moving away shyly*): I must be going.... I've been out for too long.... My parents must be worried.

Something in the girl's words shocks Franz and he stops digging. Looks up at her. She smiles at him as she more resolutely moves away.

The girl (in a forceful voice): Good-bye!

Franz (mechanically, feeling the wet sand and the hard instrument under his fingers): Good-bye!

The girl turns around and walks away. The landscape is sucking her in like a long narrow funnel. He would like to reach out with his hand for her but is afraid it will be sucked away with it.

9. das verzweiflungshotel

The light from the street came up from below although the floor the room was on was lower than the street lamps. It seemed to be coming out of hell. The name of the hotel was "Despair."

The frayed curtain on the window offered no resistance to it and the window frame cast a huge black shadow of a cross on the white ceiling. It seemed hunchbacked as everything in the room— the ceiling itself, the bed (its mattress), the furniture, the walls, the pictures on them, the floor, and he himself as well as the girl—the whore.

She was taking a piss in the chamber pot squatting on the floor by the bed on his left which was what had woken him up. He didn't feel like turning his head to look at her and saw her only with the corner of his eye but visualized her squatting down with her knees spread wide and feet splayed like a bitch relieving herself on the sidewalk. Her dark outline with the curved back and protruding head made it seem as if she really were hunchbacked. The urine striking the sides of the metal vessel made a melodious sound like the dying away of the ringing of a church bell.

But no, that was just his imagining. It was like the hissing of a snake.

The fingers of his left hand—index and middle—felt wet, almost sticky as if with oil.

He brought them to his lips and ran his tongue between them.

The liquid was watery and salty—definitely not oil. It seemed urine.

Did she piss in bed before making it to the chamber pot and he got his fingers wet in the bedclothes? She slept on his left. Or was it sweat or even tears?

No, it definitely was not sweat. It was cold in the room. And it couldn't be tears either. He never cried, not even in his sleep.

It must be urine then, her piss.

He felt with his hand the bedclothes. They were soft and rumpled and it was hard to tell if they were wet.

10. sauerbraten

The apartment reeked of sugar, spices and vinegar. Franz was making sauerbraten. The meat for the dish is normally marinated for up to four days but he got an urge for the latter in the morning and was hoping to eat it that night compensating for the shortness of time with lots of vinegar—a whole liter of it and no water or wine. That was bound to speed up the process.

Instead of beef he used horsemeat. He had recently been reading up on Hinduism and found the idea of eating cow meat offensive. Lamb was a symbol of Christ and pork was forbidden by Judaism and Islam, so lamb/mutton and pork were also out of the question. That left horsemeat. (He didn't think of goat or rabbit/hare.) Horses were noble animals, ready to serve man in any way he chose, and besides their meat was favored by nomadic people and what was he if not a modern-day intellectual nomad constantly moving about in the world of ideas. In fact the idea of sauerbraten came to him as he remembered that Asiatic nomads (Tatars) used to put chunks of horsemeat under the saddle in the morning and eat it at night without cooking. That sounded scrumptious but he couldn't fix meat in this fashion so sauerbraten was a good approximation.

As soon as he got the idea he went to the slaughterhouse and got a big chunk of horsemeat. It was fresh, the animal having been slaughtered literally minutes ago, and looked deep red with a bluish tinge like the inside of a beet. It was clearly tough so lots of vinegar would be needed. Hence a whole liter of it and no water or wine.

Franz was cleaning the apartment as he waited for the meat to marinate. He was in his underwear—white undershirt and boxer shorts—but on his feet he had his black boots with pointed toes and elastic on the sides. He also wore black socks which were held up by garters tied around his legs below the knees. He was dusting. In his right hand he carried a feather duster and in his left one a rag. The former he would fluff over carvings on furniture and complex or hard-to-get-to places and the latter would run over smooth surfaces.

Sometimes he would disappear in the walls covered with the flowery wallpaper as if in thick blue-gray clouds. Furniture would bar his way thronging annoyingly around him like kids or beggars demanding handouts at intersections. Mirrors tried to hold onto his reflection but it would always manage to escape at the last moment like a cat shying away from a hand trying to stroke it with its slinky body. A couple of times he saw his face in the mirror—the shiny black as if lacquered skull covered with the slicked-down hair with the white part line down the middle, a counterpart to the black gap between his upper two front teeth below—and he jumped back aghast his heart thumping as if from seeing a monster.

Under the varnished surfaces wood ticked away like the grandfather clock in the parlor.

As he dusted he hummed the famous drinking song over and over again:

Wer soll das bezahlen?
Wer hat das bestellt?
Wer hat so viel Pinke, Pinke?
Wer hat so viel Geld?

This meant:

Who shall pay for this?
Who has ordered it?
Who has so much green stuff, green stuff?

Who has so much dough?

When he was about half-way done with his task, while squatting down and running the duster over the bottom of the upright piano standing in the corner, in particular the foot pedals, he heard the telephone in the hallway ring. The sound was loud with every ring like the shiny metal ball in a pinball machine hitting the silence.

Franz's heart sank into the pit that suddenly opened up inside him as it seemed going all the way down to the center of the earth. Like a bolt he shot straight up and waited. The duster in his right hand was sticking up in comical fashion like the behind of an ostrich with its head in the sand and the rag hang down like the shadow of his left hand gone limp in a grotesque way.

Blood pounded in his ears and his eyesight had grown dim. The phone went on ringing. He couldn't ignore it.

Holding onto the duster and the rag as if onto the hands of two friends who had decided to stick with him come what may or those of his parents when he was a kid, he walked on tiptoes to the door and peered into the dark hallway.

At the far end of it by the outside door the telephone clung to the wall on the left like a giant rectangular tick working its way into the plaster under the wallpaper. It went on ringing.

Franz hesitated. What was he to do?

The horrible chrome-plated steel-ball sounds continued flying out of the apparatus bouncing off the wooden floor. He couldn't let this go on forever.

Still on tiptoes, staying close to the left wall, he crept forward holding onto the hands of the two friends/parents who went on sticking with him. (The duster was pointing down now trying hard to represent the shadow of his right hand gone limp but doing it in its own awkward way.)

Finally he was by the phone. The sound it made was unbearable.

He put the rag in his right hand while holding onto the duster and with his heart now in his throat reached out with his left hand for the earpiece hanging off the hook like a penis grown limp with fear, brought it to his left ear, leaned forward to the mouthpiece, and mobilizing all his strength emitted a squashed "Hello," sounding more like a death rattle than a greeting.

A tiny distant voice like the buzzing of a mechanical mosquito reached then his ear, Franz, is it you?

As he had feared, it was his wife.

II. the scream

Franz is a drawing on a page. His trunk and limbs are thin pencil lines and his head a roughly drawn circle. He is inside his house which also consists of pencil lines that constitute the edges of the adjoining planes—vertical, horizontal, and at various angles to each other. Many of these are trapezoidal and therefore he is a trapeze artist. He hangs by his hands on one of the lines representing the upper edge of the wall under the roof, holding onto it with his fingers which are also small curved pencil lines. The world is flat and white with the house a complex jumble of thin black lines.

Franz swings back and forth by moving his legs up and down. He has to gain momentum to hurl himself forward so as to grab the line corresponding to the one he hangs on way on the other side of the house. The distance is considerable and he will need a lot of momentum to reach the line. He will make himself spin around on the line he hangs on, let go of it at the proper moment, curl up into a ball, fly through the space between the two lines while spinning, reach out with his hands when he is close enough to the other line, and grab it with his hands. The task is extremely difficult but he has to carry it out. He has no choice.

He puts all his strength into moving his legs up and down and swings higher and higher. He comes up to the horizontal position on both sides. Then he goes even higher. He reaches the forty-five degree angle. The feeling is both exhilarating and frightening. He is afraid he might not be able to hold onto the line and fall. He tightens his fingers however and swings on. He almost reaches the vertical position on flying up. One more swing and he spins around the line. The feeling is only exhilarating now. He no longer is afraid of falling. He swings his legs more and spins around the line faster. He continues propelling himself with his legs and gaining speed. He spins now like a wheel in a machine. He knows now that to the outside eye he is just a blur. Still he must spin faster. The distance he has to fly through is very long. Finally he feels he has reached the right speed. When his feet are vertically down he lets go of the line, brings his legs up and his head and trunk forward, and like a ball flies spinning through the space toward the line on the other side of the house. He spins once, twice, three times, more.... He has closed his eyes and sees nothing. Finally he decides he is close enough to the other line. He opens his eyes and reaches out with his hands for the line but it isn't there. Before him everything is white. He looks down and sees nothing but whiteness below. He will fall to his death! In despair he tries to shout but he can't. He is nothing but lines. He has no mouth. Still he tries to find an opening for the feeling inside him. He collects all his strength and pushes as hard as he can.

Covered with sweat he wakes up and lets out the loudest scream of his life.

the albino syndrome

Sah ich dich wirklich nie?
Rainer Maria Rilke

I. the sea

The sea was a vast, soggy, moss-green carpet thrown over piles of things. It reeked of mold. Living creatures hid under it. You could see them stirring restlessly here and there, getting up and falling down immediately afterwards and in vain trying to change their place. Sometimes the edge of the carpet would flap up and you could catch a glimpse of the dark space under it. It was crammed with junk—broken furniture, including chairs, tables, wardrobes, beds, armchairs, and sofas, iron stoves, carts, wagons, rusty farm machinery, and things like that. Short, sturdy wooden posts were driven into the ground in a more or less regular pattern to hold up the carpet like struts it a coalmine. Bodies of large farm animals, horses, donkeys, and an occasional black and white spotted cow, could be seen here and there stretched out on their sides on the ground. There was no sight of the living creatures. They had apparently ducked quickly behind the objects scared to death of being seen by the human eye.

Sometimes a wave breaking looked white like the edge of the lower eyelid of an anemic person being pulled down by a finger.

Once a huge, dark green, almost black, fish with a long snout and sharp needle-like teeth was left stranded on the sand after a wave had broken and it frantically wiggled its way sideways down the beach until reaching the water. It looked overjoyed as it disappeared under it.

A hermit lived in an old wardrobe half-buried in a dune. Kids would sometimes open the door and he would be seen sitting on a shelf with his knees pressed to his chest staring straight ahead, his right side facing the world, all white in his loose linen clothes with which his long white hair and beard had merged so that you couldn't tell them apart. He wouldn't turn his head or say anything but merely moved his eyeballs right so that you could see his huge emerald-green right eye and press his bony index finger of his right hand to his lips asking the disturbers to be quiet. Parents would scold the children for being unruly and they would leave the man in peace for a while but eventually one of them would be unable to resist the temptation of giving in to his rebellious nature and the whole process would be repeated.

The sound of the slamming of doors continued to echo over the sand and water long after everyone had gone home and the beach was left empty.

2. summer maneuvers

The two rows of trees merged into a dot in the distance. It was as far as you could go. The cab stopped along the right side of the road and the three of them got out and crossed over to the other. The driver remained sitting high up on his seat leaning forward, his back stooping under his black overcoat, the top hat threatening to come off his head. He had stuck the whip into the bracket on his left and it drooped limply forward as if trying to imitate its master in order to ingratiate itself with him.

The road paved with crushed stone felt hard after the yielding step of the cab. The horse already stood with its head hanging down almost to the ground as if also trying to ingratiate itself with its master by previous agreement with its companion the whip.

They stopped half-way between two trees, his mother on the right, his sister in the middle, and he on the left in accordance with their age and height. He was oblivious of his sister's appearance but keenly aware of his mother's long black dress from under which showed her shiny black shoes with sharp toes, the nappy gray overcoat somewhat shorter than the dress, the matching gray scarf wrapped around her neck, and the round black hat pulled down like a pot over her ears and forehead. It was early in the morning and you could feel the cold in the air like the sharp edge of a razor pressing down on the skin. She worried constantly about her health and was prone to attacks of bronchitis and catarrhs. He also knew she was straining to see through the butterfly-like *Zwicker* glasses clamped high on the bridge of her nose, the skin around it wrinkled, her eyes narrow slits.

The mist smudged the distance. The field was enormous—a square half a mile on each side covered with short grass, perfectly flat and looking like a picture in his sister's plane geometry textbook. It was delimited on all sides by the same kind of rows of tall slender trees as those along the road. The three of them stood just to the right of one of its corners.

Way in the distance almost in the corner diagonally across from them a bunch of strange gray shapes resembling flat narrow cubes moved without any apparent reason in straight lines, at times abruptly changing direction at right angle to their original movement. Faint voices at times would come floating down from that direction unnatural tiny as if made by toys. It was soldiers drilling first thing in the morning.

The three of them stood like wooden posts driven into the ground unaware of purpose and time.

Suddenly a string of beautiful clear sounds came rolling toward them from the direction of the soldiers like beads from a breaking necklace spilling on a table. It was a bugle sounding.

The shapes stopped moving instantly and disintegrated into tiny gray dots which scattered every which way remaining however close to each other.

Suddenly again a big dot emerged out of the mess of little ones and grew bigger and bigger. A rider on a horse was galloping toward them.

Detlev's heart beat faster—his father was coming to see them. The dot grew bigger unnaturally fast and soon he could make out the black and silver helmet topped with the spear-like spike on top of his father's head, his gray uniform, the tall black boots, and the red stain of the horse's body that changed its shape as it galloped toward them. Clumps of black earth would fly at times out from under its hoofs like black birds scared off into the air.

Then his father was right in front of them huge as a building, on the horse, the spike on top of his helmet like the spire on a church. His left side was turned toward them so that he could face them better.

He sat straight in the saddle as if with a board tied to his back, his left hand in a tight black leather glove hanging low, holding the reins. The horse was restless, dancing impatiently, trying to turn around all the time, but the hand held it in place with barely a movement. The animal was no match for it.

The round monocle wedged securely in the corner of his father's left eye between the nose and the eyebrow reflected the light of the sky and looked white like an enameled metal disk. It seemed a strange eye patch as if his father were blind in that eye in a special way the normal one being when the eye patch you wear is black. His right eye could not be seen.

His torso fitted tightly inside the well-tailored tunic like his hand inside the glove. The silver insignia on his collar and shoulders shone gray in the morning light, the same color as his freshly shaven cheeks. A big pistol bulged in its black holster on his left side on the belt seemingly swollen like a badly sprained hand. A narrow band of white light like a strip of shiny metal ran down the length of the leg of his boot all the way to the spur on the heel as though both parts of a contraption for controlling the horse.

His father talked long with his mother but he was unaware of what they said as if they spoke in a language he didn't know.

Then suddenly another string of bead-like sounds came rolling toward them from the direction of the diagonally opposite corner of the field. The bugle was sounding again. The conversation stopped.

With a sharp movement of his hand his father spun the horse around and now faced them with his right side. The horse snorted and danced impatiently in one spot.

Unexpectedly his father tipped his head back, brought the fingers of his right hand dressed in the same kind of tight black leather glove as the left one to the edge of the helmet, touched it, and for the first time looked at him. His right eye looked hollow like an empty eye socket filled with darkness.

His own heart sank, a chasm opened up inside him dark like his father's right eye, and he fell into it. Still, mechanically, he raised his right hand and touched his forehead with its fingers.

His father nodded barely perceptibly, brought his right hand down, touched the horse's side with the spur, and they took off as if propelled by a catapult.

Huge clumps of black earth flew up lazily from under the horse's hoofs like big fat crows.

3. the concert

The creatures under the sea carpet were rushing madly toward the beach but would invariably fall flat on their faces before making it there. Droves upon droves of them pushed their way forward from behind the horizon and raced toward the shore, some horrible calamity clearly having taken place from where they were fleeing.

Detlev turned his head forward and stopped. Some fifty yards ahead chairs had been set up in a semicircle around the rotunda at the edge of the promenade running along the beach and people were sitting in them staring attentively ahead. Something interesting was going on inside the structure.

He resumed walking, this time at a quick pace, and, his head raised, not taking his eyes off the scene, walked around the outer row of the chairs to the left side of the rotunda and stopped next to it.

A boy about the same age as he but much frailer, completely bald and with skin white as milk, sat in the center of the rotunda on a white folding chair like one of those with people in them playing on a small white cello which he held between his legs. He was dressed in a likewise white outfit consisting of a loose shirt and baggy pants tied around his ankles. His feet were bare.

In his left hand he held a bow, once again white, and moved it vigorously across the strings while letting the fingers of his right hand travel up and down the neck of the instrument. The bow moved so violently however that it seemed it wasn't the boy's hand that was moving it but the other way around which was causing him great distress. He seemed to want to get his hand free but the bow wouldn't let it go. It was too strong for him. As to the right hand it seemed the boy was trying to catch something with its fingers on the neck of the cello but it kept hiding under the strings and getting away each time he was about grab it. The thing was too quick. It seemed clear this would go on forever and that the boy would never manage to catch the thing but he was determined not to give up.

When Detlev had first come the boy's eyes were closed but then they opened and he saw with a shock they were red like those of a white rabbit. The boy was an albino!

An expression of great pain traveled over the boy's face as he played on as it seemed because of what the bow and the thing on the neck of the instrument were doing but also because of his nature.

Deep moans, sobs, and ear-piercing screams came streaming out of the cello as the boy played, proof of the pain he was racked by.

Sometimes he would bend way down over the cello with his body limp and head swinging loose and then he would look like a martyr being taken off a cross. At other times he would lean back in the chair all tense and with elbows spread out and then it seemed he was nailed to one. There were whitecaps on the waves and as his head was seen on the background of the sea they looked like tufts of his tousled hair which was appropriately pure white.

Detlev stood with his eyes and mouth wide open unable to move. He had never seen anything similar. A profound truth had just been revealed to him whose existence he had never suspected. He had no idea what it was but knew he would have learned it sooner or later. It had something to do with the world and creatures in it and everyone had to learn it if they wanted to go on living. With a twinge of regret he realized his life would never be the same as it had been up to that instant. It had changed for good.

With time he realized he couldn't stay still forever. Sooner or later he would have to move. He turned his head right and looked at the people. They sat motionless made from the same dead substance as the world around them.

4. the meeting

The beach was empty all the way to the horizon—a narrowing white strip curving gently to the right between the flat blue of the sea on the right and the somewhat less flat green of the land on the left. The sunshine on the water was like a smile on tightly closed lips stretched from ear to ear spreading over the whole face. The last time he looked over his shoulder a few steps back the settlement was a bunch of ill-defined pale stains of the buildings among the sharp ink-black stains of the trees with the people on the beach in front of them dark poppy-seed-sized specs. He was free! They could no longer catch him and force him back to the stuffy hotel room.

Detlev walked along the edge where the surf broke and when it surged higher and spilled over his feet they looked big and clear as if seen through a magnifying glass. His arms swung rhythmically back and forth along the sides of his torso easing his walk.

Suddenly his heart sank—a pale dot appeared in the distance before him on the different shade of pale of the beach. A person was walking toward him.

His immediate reaction was to turn around and run in the direction he came from but he stopped himself immediately from doing it and went on walking. It was shameful to run.

He was afraid the person walking toward him was the albino boy he saw playing the day before and he didn't want to meet him. He had sneaked out of the room and went walking on the beach in a vague hope of meeting the boy but now that there was the possibility of this happening he no longer wanted it. There was something scary about it. If he had to meet the boy let it happen some other time but not now. He wasn't up to it at the moment.

Numb with fear he went on walking however unable to take his eyes off the figure like a rabbit charmed by a snake before being pounced on. A hope it wasn't the boy stayed on in him but was eroded gradually more and more as the figure grew nearer.

The clothes the person wore were pure white which contrasted with the yellowish white of the sand.

The person wore pants and therefore was a male. He walked on the sand so as not to get them wet. They were baggy and apparently tied around the ankles. A loose shirt completed his outfit.

It had to be the albino boy!

A floppy white hat covered the person's head—to shade it form the sun because of his sensitive skin! One more proof it was the albino boy. There could no longer be any doubt about it.

His heart was now up in his throat clutching it like an angry hand and he could barely breathe.

The boy was now some fifty yards away. He looked even smaller and frailer than the day before, pathetic on the background of the vastness of the space around him.

Detlev's blood was pounding in his ears but he walked on unable to take his eyes off the figure before him.

The boy was now some ten yards away. His features were like soot marks someone had made haphazardly all over his ghastly white face. This made him even more frightening. Was he staring him in the eye?

His hair was standing up on his head and the back of his neck felt numb.

The boy was now five, three, two, one yard away....

Had he stopped? Had he opened his mouth? Was he about to speak?

A feeling like a wild scream exploded inside his chest. The boy was too close to the edge of the surf for him to get past him comfortably so he jumped into the water and bounded like a dear through it parallel to the beach. The water reached up to his knees and he was getting wet all over but he ran on. A few more strides and he was safely past the boy. He ran back onto the sand and continued running there. Now the running was easier.

He ran for a long time but at one point felt his strength giving out. He had to slow down.

He did this and went on running. The pace felt comfortable.

After a while he realized he had slowed down again. His strength was almost gone. He couldn't go on running even at this pace much longer. He slowed down to a walk and continued walking from then on panting from exhaustion.

The outline of the next settlement rose up before him way in the distance. He had gone very far. He was safe now. Still he went on walking.

Then a thought popped up in his mind—what if the boy had decided to run after him? Was it fast footsteps he heard behind his back?

Freezing with fear he stopped and glanced over his shoulder.

The beach behind him was all clear. The boy of course didn't run after him. How could he have done that?

He relaxed, turned his head back, and went on walking. His breathing had almost returned to normal.

Another thought then popped up in his mind—what had happened to the boy? Where could he have gone to? He couldn't have made it all the way to the settlement yet.

He stopped and turned around.

For an instant he thought the beach was empty all the way to the settlement which was now like a wisp of smoke on the horizon between the sea and the land with the bathers in front of it no longer distinguishable. But then he noticed a tiny white shape some five hundred yards away standing in the water not far from where the surf reached. It was the boy. He had waded into the water up to his knees and stood looking out to sea.

Because of the distance he couldn't tell if the boy had rolled up his pants or had gone into the water with their legs down.

5. the drowning

He and the albino boy are romping around in the surf on the edge where the waves break. It is a beautiful sunny day but there appears to be no one around on the beach and in the water except the two of them. It must be early in the morning.

After a while he has had enough of just splashing around and he invites the boy to go swimming with him. The boy says he can't because he doesn't know how to swim. For an instant he feels dejected but then notices the boy's white cello lying on the sand a little higher up on the beach and he thinks it could serve as a life raft. He suggests it to the boy and the latter cheerfully agrees. He runs onto the beach, grabs the cello, and brings it into the water.

A big wave comes along, he drops the cello in the water, and throws himself down on top of it. The cello supports him well and he paddles with his hands and propels himself along away from the beach.

It is a splendid solution and he feels proud at having come up with it. He dives into the water and being an expert swimmer in a few strokes finds himself next to the boy. He tells him to paddle along and they swim next to each other.

The boy is enjoying himself tremendously and paddles furiously so that with time he himself has a hard time keeping up with him. He tells the boy to slow down but the latter doesn't listen to him and paddles furiously along.

The waves have gotten bigger and as the boy is swimming faster than he some of them soon block the sight of the former from his view. He is concerned about the boy's safety and tells him to be careful. He also yells for him to slow down.

The boy doesn't listen to him however and paddles madly along.

He glances back and sees they are a long distance away from the shore. He himself feels unsafe being so far out. He stays in place by pumping with his legs and screams at the boy to come back.

He doesn't see the boy at this instant because his view is blocked by a big wave but when it passes he sees the boy is in the water without the cello. It must have filled with water and has sunk. The solution wasn't so great after all.

His heart sinks and he screams for the boy to try staying up. He says he will come to his rescue. Then he swims as fast as he can toward the boy.

The latter stays in one place by flailing around with his arms but his head keeps going under the water and comes up only for brief instants. He is drowning.

He himself is terrified and feels guilty—it was his idea to make the boy swim on the cello. He screams again at the top of his lungs for the boy to wait for him.

It is clear the boy doesn't hear him as he is desperately trying to stay up. But still he comes up to the surface each time he goes under.

He himself swims on and hopes he will get to the boy soon.

The waves have gotten bigger however and he has difficulty swimming. Besides the distance between them has grown bigger. There must be a current that is either carrying the boy away from the shore or bringing him himself closer to it.

He doesn't give up however and keeps on swimming.

The boy is staying under the water longer and thrashes around with his arms less. His strength is giving out and he will drown if he himself doesn't reach him soon.

Then a big wave rises up between him and the boy and he cannot see the latter. When it passes the sea ahead is empty.

He screams and swims as hard as he can shouting for the boy to come up. There is no sign of him however. He has drowned.

Terrible pain seizes his heart. He is the cause of the boy's death. If it weren't for him the latter would still be alive. He screams out in boundless pain and at that instant wakes up.

6. staircase

Suddenly there was the sound of a door opening and soon after that closing. Silence followed for a few seconds and then you could hear the creaking of floorboards getting louder and louder. His mother was finally coming.

Detlev squeezed himself as far as he could into the corner and tightened his arms around his knees pressing them to his chest. He sat perfectly still and tried not to breathe. There was no need for all this because his mother wouldn't notice him even if he stood in the middle of the hallway as long as she didn't bump into him but he preferred it this way. He liked to pretend he was invisible.

The sun shone yellow through the busy floral stained glass window in the opposite wall leaving big greasy stains on the Turkish carpet on the floor.

The creaking got progressively louder and finally her figure emerged from behind the corner on the left tall and dark.

She wore a black satin gown which reached to the floor covering her feet so that her likewise black leather slippers with scuffed tops would emerge from under it only for brief instants when she brought her feet forward.

Her dark shoulder-length hair was matted and greasy apparently not having been combed that morning and not washed probably for days. Her face was yellow with deep black furrows on the forehead and around her mouth like cracks in a bar of old soap. Her eyes had sunk deep into the eye sockets but the eyeballs bulged big and round like walnuts under the eyelids which covered them tightly. Black circles ran under the eyes as if from blows. Her mouth was a thin and crooked black line. A small brown mark shaped like a tiny leach could be seen on the right side of her nose high up on the bridge left there by the *Zwicker* which she usually wore. He knew there was an identical mark on the left side.

She walked slowly, each step for her obviously an enormous effort for which she had to gather enough strength. The expression on her face wasn't pain however but boredom—boredom with what she was doing, herself, and the world.

He tried to make himself still smaller and once more not to breathe.

She was ten feet away, then five, three, two, one, and finally right in front of him. He closed his eyes and lowered his head as if she were a train rushing by just inches away.

The air stirred up by her movement brushed his face like the folds of her gown.

She had passed him.

He opened his eyes and watched her without moving his head getting farther and farther away—a foot, two, three, five, ten, until she reached the edge of the steps. There she stopped as if deliberating if she had enough strength to go down them.

She decided she did and placed her right hand on the banister.

She put her left foot on the step below and brought the right one down getting smaller as a result. Then she repeated the process and got smaller. She was descending into the wood. She continued sinking lower and lower until she was gone from his sight.

7. effi briest

Detlev and his sister Nora having breakfast in the *Orangerie* in their home which is where they usually eat in the morning. Strong sunlight forcing its way in through the tall wide windows with the glass in them clear as water in a mountain brook. Tall green plants in big clay pots all around making it seem they are out in a garden. Only the sounds of birds chirping is missing. (There are no birds in cages.) The two face each other across a rectangular table covered with a starched snow-white table cloth. It sticks its folds out along the sides on the bottom like a child its arms dressed in a heavy winter coat. The glitter of silver, glass, and white porcelain hanging above the table. Big, flat, irregular yellow stains of food (eggs) on the two plates. A small three-dimensional yellow stain of a bouquet of flowers (jonquils) in a slender glass vase hovering above it, a model for the two two-dimensional stains below which the latter unsuccessfully try to imitate.

Detlev devotes himself assiduously to the task of eating, being of the type who takes his duties seriously. His sister absentmindedly stirs around with the end of her fork in the pathetic little mound of eggs on her plate while she reads in the book that lies open on the table on her left, from time to time brings what stays on it to her lips, and deposits what comes off it in her mouth. The rest she returns to the plate.

Detlev watches what she is doing with ever increasing anger on his face. It is like a dark cloud gathering in the sky. His face literally is getting more and more dark. Finally he is unable to hold himself back and speaks staring angrily at his sister.

Detlev *(testily)*: How long are you going to read this stupid *Effi?* You've been reading it for the past five years. You must know it by heart.

His sister pays no attention to him and goes on reading and stirring the food on the plate with the end of her fork.

Detlev *(angrier)*: For God's sake! You'll become like her... crazy.... You'll die in the end too for no reason whatever....

There is still no response form his sister. She appears to be deaf.

Detlev *(turning red in the face)*: You must be doing it so as to eat less! You want to starve yourself to death. You're anorexic.... Skin and bones.... No wonder they called you Nora.... You're aNORAexic....

His words have hit a raw nerve in his sister. Her behavior changes dramatically. In an instant she becomes energetic, turns red in the face like a mirror image of her brother, stops reading, and stares angrily at him her eyes bulging.

Nora *(through clenched teeth)*: Look who's talking! It wasn't me who tried killing herself by jumping out the window!

Detlev (redder and angrier): I didn't jump out the window! I fell! I wanted to see what was under the bushes and leaned out too far!

Nora (derisively): Leaned out too far.... A likely story.... Everyone knows you jumped out. If it weren't for those bushes you would have broken your neck and died!

Detlev (sees his chance): The bushes.... You think I would have tried to kill myself by jumping out the window with bushes under them? I would have found another one... with stones under it....

Nora (dismissive): With stones under it.... Where would you have found a window with stones under it when there were only two windows in the room and they both faced the same way and had bushes growing under them? Besides there were no stones under the window anywhere around that hotel. You did it to imitate that albino boy who drowned because of feeling guilty about not talking to him when you saw him on the beach.... You said so yourself.... So that's why you did it. You wanted to die like him!

Detlev (angrily and at the same time defensively): I didn't want to die!... I said I felt guilty because I thought he drowned the day I saw him... when he went into the water.... But then I found out he drowned two days later.... It was an accident.... He didn't kill himself because I didn't stop to talk to him. He went into the water early in the morning when there was no one on the beach and he didn't know how to swim.... So why should I have felt guilty?... *(Sees a chance to change the subject he doesn't like.)* Anyway that was years ago but you're starving yourself now.... Look at yourself!.... You look just like aunt Nora did before she died.... No wonder they named you after her.... You got it from mother's side of the family.

8. the hare

Detlev rolled the body over with his foot. Its back and sides were a beautiful gray-brown, the color of the woods on the horizon, and the belly pure white like the snow under his feet. There was no sign of the bullet hole and he squatted cradling the light Flaubert rifle in the crook of his left arm and turned the body over farther with his hand. A tiny red dot on the white snow appeared where the blood had sunken in, incongruously small and pale, inappropriate to the event that had produced it. He had expected it to be big and dark, almost black. There was no sign of the bullet hole. He looked for it on the head which is what he had aimed for but it wasn't there. He searched with his fingers through the fur and finally found it. It was lower down on the shoulder—a small wet red spot among the blood-matted fur and not a black round hole, the kind through which a soul can escape as he would have expected as a little boy. "A black round hole through which a soul can escape," he thought smiling bitterly. How different he was now!

His face darkened and he turned the body over once more. The head lay flat on the ground with the eye staring vertically into the sky. It was round and black but not at all like a hole through which a soul can escape—beautiful and mysterious like water under the ice in a half-frozen brook. The fact it was beautiful disturbed him and he stood up lifting the hare by its hind legs.

They turned out to be unexpectedly big and the body long and heavy—the head lay on the ground when he held the animal in his hand. He couldn't carry it like that all the way home but would have to sling it over his shoulder. This would mean his clothes might get stained with blood. He had thought the cook would prepare it in a marinade and was looking forward to the meal but now the idea made him sick. He felt physically nauseous as if having tasted the dish and finding it revolting.

He opened his hand and let the body fall down to the ground. It slid along his boot leg and arranged itself snugly around his foot as if trying to keep it warm.

He moved the foot quickly away and walked off.

The sky was uniformly lead-gray which seemed appropriate for the way he felt—a heavy weight pressing down on him from above.

The snow was deep in places and his feet would sink then up to his knees. He could have avoided the drifts but walked in a straight line toward the road framed on both sides by the slender leafless trees.

He climbed up the escarpment, got onto the road, and turned left. It was much easier walking now with the hard-packed snow on top of the crushed-stone surface. He continued cradling his rifle in the crook of his arm like a baby since it didn't have a strap.

For a short while he walked absentmindedly but then his eyes focused on the road ahead and his heart sank. Way in the distance where the two lines of trees met a tiny pale dot was moving up and down and from side to side—a person was walking toward him.

He was sure the person was the albino boy he had seen playing the cello on the promenade by the sea way back then grown to be almost a man now, the same age as he. He knew the boy had drowned but at that moment it didn't count. Somehow he has turned out to be alive. Maybe he didn't drown after all or was reincarnated but at any rate was now walking toward him.

He didn't know why he was afraid but the fear was overwhelming. All he could think of was turning around and running as fast as he could down the road or even better veering off and cutting through the snowy fields to the distant gray-brown woods on the horizon.

But he kept on walking forward. There was no way he could flee. Men in his family never ran away from anything.

Stiff as if wooden he walked on unable to take his eyes off the figure before him moving up and down and from side to side growing bigger and bigger with each step destined to meet him.

It was definitely a man and he was dressed in light clothes—not white but gray or pale blue.

The man walked in a determined way swinging his arms to ease his walking.

He wore tall black boots and had a cap on his head.

There was a black strap running across his chest. Was he carrying a cello in its case on his back?

No there was no neck sticking out above the shoulder.

That didn't matter.

The man was now some hundred yards away.

His clothes were pale blue and seemed some kind of a uniform. That also didn't matter. His face was a white stain between his cap and the collar of his coat. He was an albino.

It was seconds before they would meet.

The hair on his head stirred trying to stand up, his neck felt numb, and his throat dry so that it stuck together. He had to produce some saliva to unstick it. His heart skipped a beat and his eyesight grew dim. He was going to faint!

The man was now some twenty yards away and he realized it was the postman in his uniform and with his mail bag hung across his chest making his rounds on foot walking from one village to the next.

He breathed easier but still was barely able to say, *Grüss Gott!* in reply to the man's greeting as they passed each other.

9. the club

Detlev dreams he walks into a room. It is big but cozy with a low ceiling, dark walls with pictures hanging on them, a thick carpet on the floor, and heavy dark-wood furniture. Soft light from gas lamps on the walls illuminates the room just right so that it feels homey but not dark. It must be at night.

The place has to be a club of some kind and he either is its member or has a chance of becoming one. There are men standing around in pairs or larger groups talking and drinking from mugs or glasses in their hands.

A waiter, young, tall, and dressed in a black suit and white shirt with a black tie walks up to him and offers him a drink in a heavy mug he is holding on a tray. He picks it up, thanks the waiter, and brings the mug to his lips. Warmth and a pleasant aroma flows from it—it is *Glühwein*, a drink he loves. He sips from the mug and savors the warmth and taste of the beverage. It is delicious.

He decides he wants to see more of the room and so strolls through it sipping on the drink from time to time.

He feels comfortable in the surroundings. The men are all dressed in uniforms, in tight-fitting tunics, riding britches, and tall boots, some of them with pistols inside holsters on their belts, other with short ornamental daggers, and a few with long sabers that dangle obediently along their sides. They all have closely clipped hair and stand straight and stiff like military men are trained to do. Some have monocles over their eyes. They appear to belong to the class of Junkers the same as his family.

He feels still more comfortable in the surroundings, practically at home. It is as if he realized only now that he is a member of the club or can become one if he only wants to. In other words it is only his wish that stands in the way of his becoming a member if he isn't one already.

He stops for a moment and then a man, older than he but in the prime of his life, comes up to him and greets him. He greets the man back and the two talk.

The man is also drinking *Glühwein* and they comment on the excellence of the drink. Then they express their admiration for the place, the people in it, and so forth. The conversation moves along these lines and then the man suggests they sit down at one of the tables. It is big but there is no one sitting at it and they sit down at one of its corners at right angles to each other and continue talking as before.

They both finish their drinks at the same time and the waiter instantly appears from somewhere with two new full mugs on the tray. He and the man take them, the waiter takes the empty mugs away, and the conversation continues.

It turns out the man is an army officer and like his own father had been bringing his family to a seaside resort when he was on summer maneuvers.

He is excited by this discovery and wants to find out if the man had been bringing his family to the same place his own had been going to but at that instant he hears a loud noise coming from the corner of the room on his right. The man sits on his left.

He turns his head right to see what has happened but notices nothing unusual there. It is not surprising though because the men standing in groups block his view of the corner. This is where the noise seems to have come from. It had sounded like a pistol shot and he concludes someone must have accidentally shot off his gun. Apparently it didn't cause any damage because the men stand talking as if nothing has happened. He is satisfied with the explanation and turns his head back.

When he does this he finds the man lying face-down on the table. He is surprised because the man didn't act drunken at all just seconds ago. Did he suddenly fall asleep on him? That wouldn't make any sense. The man has been so polite and friendly and falling asleep in these circumstances would be rude.

Curious, he taps the man on the back but the latter doesn't react. He shakes him gently but the latter still shows no sign of life. He decides to see what has happened to the man and tries to lift him up and turn him over.

He manages to do that but the man slips off the chair and falls down on the floor face up. The chair falls over too and makes it easier for him to see.

The man's eyes are wide open, their irises nearly hidden under the forehead. His head is turned right and a dark stream of blood flows out of the temple onto the cheek and the collar. Detlev wants to see what the hole the bullet made looks like so he bends down and examines it. It is perfectly round and black—empty. All the blood has flowed out of it while the man lay on the table.

He moves his eyes away and notices there is a pistol lying on the floor next to the man's left hand. The man clearly shot himself

with it—committed suicide—while he had looked away. The fact
he didn't hear the shot doesn't surprise him. It is as if the noise
that had made him turn his head away originally were enough. It
could have been an echo of the pistol shot that killed him.

He doesn't question himself why the man committed suicide and
feels no sorrow at the fact. It is as if such acts were an everyday
occurrence and you didn't have to worry yourself about them. It
is as if dying were an everyday occurrence.

He doesn't like the way the man is lying however and he
rearranges the body so that it looks more comfortable. He is
careful not to stain his hands with blood.

Then he stands up and looks around.

The room is much smaller now, the size of a normal bedroom,
and totally empty of people and furniture. Everyone had cleared
out and the furniture was removed while he was attending to the
man.

10. *graf von toten tieren*

The gray cord piping on his gray tight-fitting *heyduck* jacket moved
past the bare tree branches on the background of the cloudy sky as

if past itself—gray on gray past gray on gray. Giving in to an unstoppable urge to be among trees he was walking through an orchard. He was Detlev Graf von Kalckreuth now.

They carried his father clumsily, his left arm hanging down, the hand dragging on the floor lifeless but at times when it hit an obstacle jumping around frantically as if looking for something it had lost but which it desperately needed—along the thick florid Turkish carpet, the polished wood floor, brown and shiny like the surface of a stagnant pond, and down the steep staircase, gradually deeper and deeper into the wood until he and his carriers disappeared in it.

One of the carriers accidentally let go of his right leg on the staircase and the whole procession nearly went tumbling down, a cascade of flesh and bones spilling over the wooden rapids.

They had wrapped a bandage around his head, uselessly, for he was dead by then, and blood seeping through the white cloth on the left temple formed a big red stain like a cherry squashed by an angry foot.

He was aware now of the rhythmic motion of his own limbs, relaxed, self-assured, like those of people indifferent to their surroundings, feeling themselves remote from and superior to them, unthreatened, capable of handling anything that might come their way.

You're a born leader of men, a ruler, everyone told him. Just like your father. You even look like him... exactly... spit and image of when he was young.

Exactly like... spit and image?.... No, he was not. He was very different. Even his body was different. His hands were soft with long fingers like those of a pianist and his father's hard and stiff as if cut out from a wooden board. He remembered walking down the street with his father holding his hand when he was little. It felt like a piece of wood and he was scared to death it would slip out from his grip and he would be left alone. It was cold and hard as if cut out from a wooden board too when he kissed it for the last time before they closed the coffin.

Fingers long like those of a pianist.... Maybe he should have become a pianist to concert around with that poor albino cellist boy.... But that would have been impossible since the boy had drowned.

It was too late now anyway. What he was could not be changed.

He realized he walked due north. If he continued eventually he would come to the sea. He recalled it had looked sometimes like a vast soggy moss-green carpet. He imagined himself lying on the ground under it among rusty junk of every kind and bodies of large farm animals—horses, donkeys, and an occasional black and white spotted cow.

II. der fangschuss

The gray stretched into the distance like a file of his classmates standing at attention during the morning roll call. It was only after a while that Detlev realized it was the ceiling above him which he was staring at as he lay on his back. It was very early, probably before five in the morning. He could hear his friend Volker breathing heavily on his left. The others were too far away to be heard. None of them snored at this time. His bed was in the very corner.

And then he remembered the dream which he had just had and which had woken him up.

He is at the seaside resort where they used to spend summer holidays when he was little, running up the steps to the Werther Hotel. He must have just arrived from the station in a cab and is hurrying although he doesn't know why.

He runs inside and finds himself in the lobby which is full of people, as it appears young men like he, standing around, singing, drinking, and in general making merry. The place is lit up (he remembers it was dark outside) and there are wreaths of pine branches and evergreens hanging on the walls and lying on tables as at Yuletide. It must be the holiday season for he realizes he is warmly dressed although he is not wearing an overcoat.

He stops as he rushes in for he doesn't know where to go and at that instant a man, about his age, height, and build comes up to him laughing and gesticulating with his hands in one of which he is holding a heavy mug with something steamy in it. The man puts his free left arm around his shoulders and says he is very glad he has finally come.

The man is dressed in a loose red satin outfit consisting of a long shirt and baggy pants tied at the ankles somewhat like those clowns wear and on his head has a tasseled red velvet cap trimmed with white rabbit fur but his face is pure white and his eyes shine red like rubies. He realizes then who the man is—the albino boy from his childhood. He has drowned in reality but in the dream it doesn't matter. He has grown up to be a man and has come to welcome him.

The man slaps him on the back and lets him sniff the mug. He says he is drinking *Glühwein* and that it is delicious. His breath smells of the drink. He suggests they get a drink for him. The aroma of the beverage is wonderful and he agrees to the suggestion.

They walk to the bar which is in the back of the room. The man puts his hand on his back at times to push him along and he feels good about it. It is good to be on friendly terms with someone knowledgeable. They have to fight their way through the throng of people who have gathered around the bar but in the end they are there. There happen to be two empty stools standing at it and they sit down on them he on the right and the man on the left.

There are a couple of waiters behind the counter and the man motions to the one who is closer for him to bring them another drink. The bartender does this quickly and he himself takes the mug and savors the heavy heady potion. It tastes delicious.

He feels great about being with the man. He had waited for this all his life from the moment when he saw him playing in the rotunda on the promenade by the sea and finally his wish has come true. They talk about all sorts of unimportant things, reminiscing about events from their past as if they really know each other since childhood.

Then the situation becomes unclear as if he had passed out and came to again. Two steaming mugs stand in front of them on the counter, they drink out of them, laugh, and converse in slurred speech. They are both very drunk.

He notices then a big pistol—a Mauser—lying on top of the counter next to the man's mug. He didn't notice it before and doesn't know how it got there. He is intrigued by it, reaches out with his right hand, and takes it. It is heavy and makes him feel good as if he held on to a hand of someone bigger and stronger than he who would protect him. He weighs the pistol in his hand and then unexpectedly to himself presses its barrel to his right temple.

It feels hard and cold and he takes it away instantly and puts the pistol back on the counter.

The man then twists his head toward him bending down a little and looks in his eyes asking silently if he would like him to do it. He knows what "it" means and shakes his head affirmatively.

The man says something back to him which he doesn't understand because of the noise in the room and because of the latter's slurred speech except for one word which he hears very clearly—*Fangschuss*—*coup de grace.*

He knows that the man has asked if he would like him to shoot him and answers without hesitation that he would.

The man picks up the pistol with his left hand, puts his right arm around his neck, pulls him toward himself, tells him to close his eyes, and presses the barrel to his left temple.

He feels the man's strong arm on his neck, warmth streaming from his face toward his own, and the cold barrel of the pistol pressing against his skin, is comforted by it, closes his eyes, and hears a soft whooshing sound like something fuzzy flying through the air and assumes it is the bullet entering his brain. In an instant everything turns gray which surprises him because he had thought it would become black. The grayness continues and he concludes that being dead isn't bad at all.

karla and georg or the

ambiguous nature of clouds

In memoriam K. G.

I. in bed

Georg lay on top of the bed in his dormitory room sleeping. The bed was a steel-and-concrete cantilever platform its head attached to the middle of one of the inside walls, with a thin horsehair mattress over it. White sheets, a small square pillow, and a thick gray wool blanket constituted its bedclothes.

The room was cubical with rough gray stucco over concrete walls, a small rectangular window in the middle of the outside wall, and a narrow gray metal door in the middle of the one opposite it. A shallow gray metal wardrobe stood in the corner on the left of the bed looking like a man with a flat chest and narrow shoulders doing all he could to make himself unnoticed. (He seemed successful in his endeavor.) A stool consisting of a platform similar to that of the bed was located directly to the left of the wardrobe, Georg's clothes—gray pants and a white shirt—thrown carelessly over and his shoes and socks carelessly under it. A small rectangular plain pinewood table, its top clear of things, and a matching chair next to it stood against the wall facing the bed and directly opposite it.

Georg lay curled up on his right side his arms crossed on his chest and knees pressed against them, almost completely covered by the blanket so that only his tousled dark hair stuck out from under it like the curled-up fingers of the raised hands of an excited crowd. A not quite full moon, cubical like a cardboard box with its top partly open, hung in the empty sky its light like soiled white underwear spilling out of it. It penetrated into the room through the window and seemed scattered over Georg's body, some of the items appearing to have gotten torn on barbed wire they encountered on their way down.

Karla slept across the wall from Georg in a room constructed and apportioned exactly like that of Georg's except being the mirror image of it, the platform of the bed in it constituting the extension of that in Georg's. (Metal beams twice the length necessary for one bed were used in the construction extending from one room to the other and it was the advantage this offered that was the principal cause for the mirror-image relationship between the two rooms.) No clothes or shoes were visible anywhere in Karla's room, she having put them away in the wardrobe before going to bed being an exceptionally neat person unlike Georg.

Karla lay on her left side in a position identical to that of Georg's, covered up the same as he almost to the top of her head with the blanket so that she also looked like a mirror image of him unable to avoid obeying the mirror-image relationship principle between the two rooms. Only her straight mousy hair appeared unwilling or unable to obey the rules.

The light the moon cast in Karla's room was different from that in Georg's however. Scattered over her small sleeping figure it looked like a bouquet of white roses someone had thrown on top of the blanket. The roses appeared to be past their prime but bore no trace of having come in contact with barbed wire.

Strictly speaking Georg and Karla slept in separate rooms on separate beds but because of the physical circumstances they seemed to be lying in one bed—a pair of Siamese twins joined at the head, their dreams crossing freely from one brain to the other like museum visitors strolling from room to room looking with interest at the pictures on the walls.

2. in the field

It was the height of spring. Sounds were coming from the houses ringing the huge flat square field—doors and windows opening and closing during spring cleaning, pots banging in the kitchens during cooking and cleaning up, mattress springs creaking as people lying on top of them made love. Men were digging up yards in preparation for spring planting and making holes to put posts in. Plants were straining to grow like constipated people trying to move their bowels, grains of sand were being pushed aside, blades of grass were giving out soft "Aaahs" in amazement as they peeked above the ground for the first time.

Clouds were moving every which way in the pristine blue sky.

Karla watched two of them nearing each other about to collide.

Look Georg, she said, They're about to collide.

They won't collide, Georg laughed. They will join up and become one.

They will permeate each other, Karla conceded, And then become a bigger whole.

Yes, Georg agreed.

Georg, Karla said enthusiastically, Let's go to the opposite ends of the field and run like crazy toward each other and then merge into a new big whole.

Georg thought it was a great idea and agreed readily.

But don't stop at the last moment or veer off to the side, Karla admonished him. We have to collide, I mean merge.

I won't, I promise, Georg assured her.

And we must run real fast, Karla insisted.

I will, Georg assured her once again.

They went to the opposite ends of the field and could barely see each other. Karla yelled something, Georg heard her voice like a torn-off corner of a sheet of paper flying in the wind and took off like a bat out of hell seeing Karla do the same at that very moment. They ran straight toward each other.

Karla's small body with its short legs and a big head looked unequal to the difficult task imposed on it but it was doing better than expected. Georg was amazed at how fast she ran and felt he couldn't be outdone by her so he pushed himself to the limit. He was covering the ground in giant strides like a horse, his arms swinging way up forward and then back, his lungs seeming on fire like the engine of a plane going down.

They were getting closer and closer.

Georg saw the floppy black warm-up pants flap on Karla's legs doing their utmost to help her and her bare arms swing up and down like his along her chest covered with a black ribbed sleeveless sweater its turtle-neck collar pushing up her chin. Her fists were two white mysterious devices helping her move faster.

They were twenty yards apart, then fifteen, ten, five, four, three, two, one.... Things got dark, their chests nearly touched, Georg rotated in the counterclockwise direction and so did Karla, they threw their arms around each other, fell over, and rolled in the direction he had been running. (He was fifty percent heavier than she.)

They kept on rolling, holding onto each other and laughing until coming to a stop with him on top of her.

His eyes were shut but he found her mouth with his, opened her lips with his tongue, and penetrated inside feeling her cool smooth teeth and wet gums. All of a sudden she was perfectly still like a flower devoting all of its attention and energy to blooming.

3. a poem

A budding young poet by the name of Georg von Tarnow was walking along the street that ran past the field just at that instant. He was of medium height and build, had long dark wavy hair, a smooth and swarthy Indian-looking face that many girls found attractive, and was dressed in fashionable baggy gray pants and a loose white shirt with an open collar which billowed in the air as he walked.   He was enjoying the sight of the field and the buildings around it and the following poem formed itself instantly in his mind:

spring
is the cause of itself
water
unties its tight knots
plants
stand up on their toes
to see themselves grow tall
the sun
goes playing by itself
in the empty sandbox
of the sky
boys
fly huge plots of land

instead of kites.

4. karla cooks

Kids were playing hide-and-seek outside under the windows. One of them, a scrawny boy of about ten, red-haired, pug-nosed, with freckles like flyspecks on a mirror around his narrow snake-like eyes and two of his front teeth missing, was rattling off a verse for counting participants out who stood in a circle around him. It went as follows:

Eins zwei, drei, vier, fünf, sechs, sieben,
Meine Mutter kocht rote Rüben,
Meine Mutter kocht Speck,
Und du gehst weg.

This meant:

One, two, three four, five, six, seven,
My mother cooks beets,
My mother cooks bacon,
And you go out.

The person chosen went out, the verse was repeated, and the one left in the end was to look for the others.

Karla's face lit up like a lantern when she heard the words *rote Rüben* (beets) and *Speck* (bacon).

Georg, she shouted, I have an urge to cook a beet-and-bacon soup. Let's go and get some ingredients and cook it together.

Georg was always ready to do what came into Karla's head and agreed with enthusiasm.

Karla had never cooked anything before and had never had or heard of a beet-and-bacon soup but she instantly formed a plan for what the soup should taste and look like and, being an extremely methodical person, made a mental list of things she would need. It was the following:

- 4 beets
- 3 tomatoes
- 4 potatoes
- ½ cabbage
- 3 carrots
- 1 onion
- 1 head of garlic
- ½ pound of bacon
- 1 jar of sour cream
- 1 bunch of parsley

The two of them ran down to the nearby grocery store, got the things, and on coming home went to the communal kitchen, got a big pot and a skillet, and started cooking. Karla was deciding on the spur of the moment what to do, doing much of the work herself and telling Georg how to help her. He obediently followed her instructions.

They peeled the potatoes, filled the pot half full with water, and put in it two of the potatoes and the four unpeeled beets minus the greens to cook for twenty minutes.

Then they cut up the bacon into fine cubes and fried it in the skillet with the onion.

They poured off some of the fat, added shredded cabbage, and finally chopped tomatoes.

When the potatoes and beets had cooked enough they took them out and put into the liquid the stuff that had been fried in the skillet.

They mashed up the two potatoes with a little sour cream, put them back in the pot, sliced up the carrots and the remaining two potatoes and put them also in the pot together with the beet greens.

When the stuff in the pot had cooked for half an hour they added the beets, peeled and chopped up, and cooked the whole thing for another half an hour.

At that time they added four crushed garlic cloves, a handful of chopped parsley, some salt and pepper, and let it stand for a few hours. It turned gradually more and more red and in the end developed a deep red color like a choice Bordeaux.

Karla tasted the soup when it appeared to be done and screwed up her face as she was bending over the pot, the spoon under her mouth. She scooped up another spoonful and offered it to Georg asking him what he thought.

The soup tasted wonderful to him and he told her so.

No, Karla said. What it needs is some dill and sour cream.

Most of the latter was still intact in the jar but she thought they would need more to have with the soup over the days it would take them to finish it.

She asked Georg to fetch the two items from the store while she cleaned up in the kitchen, he did it with enthusiasm, and when he came back they sat down at the table to enjoy the fruits of their hard labor. (They had spent almost three hours cooking.)

They ate the soup with chopped dill and a dollop of sour cream in each plate and it tasted wonderful, getting better and better with time. (It took them three days to finish it.)

The experience was the beginning of Karla's very successful amateur culinary career. The soup became known as *"Karlas rote Rüben und Speck Eintopf"* (Karla's beet-and-bacon whole-meal soup) and a favorite with their families and friends.

5. karla sings
(the no-penny opera)

The party was given by the three monkeys—Monikas—Monika 1, Monika 2, and Monika 3. They welcomed their guests appropriately seated on the sofa facing the door with their legs crossed—Monika 1 covering her eyes, Monika 2 with index fingers stuck in her ears, and Monika 3 with the stiff white fingers of her hand like the claws of a she-bear over her mouth.

It was a potluck party and people brought what they liked the most or knew how to make.   Hungarians brought their spicy goulash, Poles the savory *bigos*, Ruthenians the scrumptious chicken Lemberg, and Russians the salty "piss" soup *(shchi)*. Karla and Georg brought Karla's famous beet-and-bacon whole-meal soup which turned out to be one of the favorites. Playing up their pretended African heritage the three monkeys had prepared fish baked with shaved coconut and bananas accompanied by tapioca pudding and served drinks with tropical ingredients in them such as pineapple juice, mango juice, and coconut milk.

A lot of singing went on during the party with the following song hands down the most popular.

Alle Rosen duften, alle Rosen duften,
Nur die Mat(t)rosen duften nicht.
Alle Fische schwimmen, alle Fische schwimmen,
Nur die Backfische schwimmen nicht.

This meant:

All roses smell nice, all roses smell nice,
Only dead roses/sailors don't smell nice.
All fishes can swim, all fishes can swim,
Only baked fishes/teenage girls cannot swim.

Someone started singing the song first when people were having the baked fish dish and discovered that his/her glass was empty. Everyone joined in and pointed vigorously at their glasses—empty or not so empty—while singing the line about baked fishes not swimming. After that the song would be started up again by anyone whenever he or she had run out of drink with the rest of the crowd dutifully joining in. (People invariably held their noses while singing the line about the sailors not smelling nice.)

Everyone had a terrific time and the party lasted far into the night.

The high point of the party and its culmination was the performance of an opera called *Manon, Let's Go!* patterned on Puccini's *Manon Lescaut*, advertised as the shortest opera ever. It was subtitled *Die Keinegroschenoper (The No-penny Opera)* because, it being so short, people didn't have to pay to see it.

It featured Karla and her (everyone's) friend the Hungarian Laszlo and went as follows:

Laszlo and Karla come crawling out of the kitchen on their knees, their clothes in disarray, and with great difficulty get up on their feet in the middle of the room. Laszlo then sings some wild aria, a mixture of *bel canto*, a German cabaret song, and Hungarian folk music which lasts about thirty seconds. He stops and Karla opens her mouth wide and sings a desperate, ear-piercing, high C++ (high E?) note. Laszlo instantly grabs her by her hand, shouts "Manon, let's go!" and pulls her away into the crowd.

People laughed their heads off (English was understood by everyone) and the performance was repeated a dozen times, at first with the original singers and then with different people trying their hand (throat) at the easy art of opera singing.

6. two Japanese poems

Karla saw a sheet of paper folded in two lying in the grass before her. She came up to it, bent down, picked it up, unfolded it, and saw it contained the following two paragraphs of numbers:

45788233200300734
90780809234
523476986876837

2345234808
86876708023753
08702347982348992346

Look Georg, she said excited, It's two poems.

Georg looked at the page and then at Karla.

These are not poems, he said in disbelief. These are just a bunch of numbers.

No, Karla said earnestly. These are Japanese poems.

Look, she went on, pressing against him and pointing with her finger first to the first set of numbers and then to the second, This one speaks of purple plum tree petals lying on silver steps in the dusk, and this one about teary eyes watching Mount Fuji during a snowstorm. Can you see it?

Georg studied the numbers carefully for a long time and thought he sensed something similar to what Karla had said forming itself in his mind but it never coalesced fully for him.

No Karla, he finally said with sadness, I really don't. I just see numbers.

7. soufflé

The woman had come into the bar carrying two canvas bags stuffed full to the point of bursting and Georg wasn't sure if she was traveling someplace and had a stopover or was a bag lady. She appeared to be in her late fifties or early sixties, was short, heavyset, with a fat pasty face and thin lank hair of uncertain color—was it blond or gray?—and was dressed in worn baggy clothes. Georg found her ugly.

She sat at the far end of the table next to his so that they were nearly two tables apart and in order to make himself heard properly he had to speak to her in a raised voice. Throughout the conversation he had a feeling he was shouting at her in anger. She likewise spoke in a loud voice to him and it looked as if the two were having it out in front of everyone in the bar.

She had complained to the waiter about the price of the glass of beer she had ordered saying it was outrageous but in the end capitulated and paid up. She continued grumping about the price however and each time she brought the glass to her lips would scrunch up her face as if she were about to take a swig of vinegar instead of beer.

Out of compassion Georg had voiced support for the way she felt about the price of the beer after she had asked him what he thought of it and she continued talking to him after that. She rambled on about all sort of unconnected things and he mostly said nothing.

Then at one point, out of nowhere, she said, Why don't you come to my place? I will give you a *soufflé*.

Georg was startled—*soufflés* are prepared and not given. And why was she being so chummy all of a sudden? He found the prospect of going to her place unpleasant. (It turned out she was neither in transit nor a vagrant.) He was allergic to eggs however and found a simple way of declining her offer. He told her he couldn't have eggs.

She wasn't talking about eggs, the woman laughed, but about sex.

About sex? Georg asked startled even more. He had no idea what the woman was talking about.

Yes sex, the woman laughed. She was prepared to give him oral sex. That's what "*soufflé*" meant.

He was shocked by what she said, even more, it seemed, by the fact that "soufflé" referred to oral sex than by the nature of her offer.

He had no idea "soufflé" could mean oral sex, he said. He had always heard it called Schwanzlutschen (tail sucking).

Schwanzlutschen? The woman laughed. She had heard it called many things but never that. It must be a kids' term, she went on. Did he ever have oral sex?

No, he didn't, Georg replied blushing. (He had been too bashful to ask the women he had been with for such a risqué practice.)

Well, this was his chance, the woman replied. She would initiate him to it. Did he want her to?

No, Georg replied, disgust rising up in him. He was already attached to someone else.

Attached to someone? The woman laughed. What did it matter? The girl wouldn't have to know.

No, Georg insisted, this time with clear anger in his voice. He didn't want to.

Alright, the woman said grumpily. He didn't have to take her up on her offer. He had seemed like a nice fellow so she just had wanted to do something for him. She wouldn't even have charged him that much.

8. karla dances

The performance took place in an abandoned factory converted into an auditorium, in the evening, with the dusk falling reluctantly outside.

The audience sat on the floor on things they had brought along—stools, cushions, blankets, boxes, pots, books, etc., or simply on the bare floor.

Karla danced in front of a big electric motor painted silver to which a huge airplane propeller, also painted silver, had been attached, arranged in such a way that it tilted at regular intervals from one side to the other and forwards and backwards, all against the background of the tall windows caked with a gray layer of dust and industrial effluents from the time the factory was operational.

As Karla went through the abstract machine-like ("industrial") movements she moved across the floor in such a way as to put herself in danger of being hit by the rapidly rotating blades that swung blindly back and forth. Each time she did this she came unbelievably close to being injured but always prevented this from happening by getting out of the way in time. This made the spectacle very suspenseful especially since much of the time she danced facing the audience unable to see what was happening behind her.

Karla was totally naked, covered with a layer of paint she prepared herself from various ingredients including lead and mercury, with potassium permanganate sprinkled on top. The tiny purple crystals sparkled beautifully on the silvery paint like stars in a nonrealistic, fairytale sky. Karla had smeared her head, armpits, and pubic region with Vaseline and put the paint over it so that it looked as though she had shaved off all of her hair.

The dance was performed to the monotonous humming of the motor and Karla's own breathing which got progressively louder and raspier from fatigue as she went on. With time too Karla began perspiring and the sweat made the potassium permanganate crystals melt and run in rivulets down her skin looking like so many tiny square eyes crying lilac tears in anticipation of something terrible that was to come.

The audience was put on edge by the dance and gasps of fear and relief would burst out at times from between its collective lips as Karla first subjected herself to and then escaped the terrible danger. At the beginning her name was called out a few times but soon that stopped as people were warned this might make Karla lose her concentration and get hurt.

One of the persons guilty of calling out "Karla!" naturally was Georg and he wanted to do it a few times after hearing the warning but each time stopped himself from shouting by stifling his voice and putting his hand over his mouth. When the dance ended his legs shook so hard he could barely stand up and he was no less drenched with sweat than Karla.

The giant violets of dusk were determined to find out how Karla was doing by peering in through the windows throughout the whole dance but their view was blurred by the layer of dirt caked on the panes.

9. a promise

Promise me, Karla said to Georg, You will marry Monika 3 when I'm no longer around.

Georg was astounded.

When you're not around? He asked. Where are you going?

Nowhere, Karla answered. It's just a hypothetical request. Just in case. Everyone has to go one day and so will I. So in case I'm gone please marry Monika 3. Won't you Georg? She loves you, I know.

Has she told you that? Georg asked surprised.

No, but I can tell, Karla answered. Women can tell things like that. You men will never understand it.

Won't you? Karla asked again as Georg remained silent.

But I don't love her, he answered.

I know you don't, Karla said, And I hope you won't. But she loves you and if I'm not around then what harm would it do? You could think about me when the two of you make love and it would be as if it were us.

You are a tragic figure Karla, Georg said. You upset me.

Tragic-shmagic, said Karla. Tragic figures died with the ancient Greeks. I'm a modern emancipated woman and that's all. It isn't much but it's all I can be.

So, how about it Georg? She pressed on. Will you marry her?

I'm not going to marry anybody! Georg said angrily. I'm not getting tied down!

Then at least go and live with her, Karla said. That would be good enough.

Live with her?! Georg exploded. And have the other two Monikas around me day and night?

But it would be as if you two lived alone, Karla persisted. You know those two don't meddle into other people's business... don't see or hear anything. And if you're worrying what people would say... about you and Monika 3 getting together... she won't tell anyone. You know how well she keeps a secret.

Leave me alone, Georg said angrily. He was getting very uneasy with the subject and was fidgeting around in his clothes as if in an uncomfortable chair.

Georg!? Karla pressed on more firmly.

No! Georg said angrily.

Just promise me you will consider it, Karla pleaded.

Georg stayed silent.

Georg, please! Karla pressed on. Just consider it.... Yes?

Yes, Georg said grudgingly after a while just to get rid of her. I
will consider it. Does it make you happy?

Yes, Karla said, an expression of relief like a drop of oil on water
spreading over her face.

10. three indian poems

Georg sat down and in one fell swoop wrote the following three
poems which he considered Indian.

1.

Notshiva
of too many arms

their angular movements

make me yearn

for the still waters of the Ganges

2.

the soft scimitars

of your arms

slice up my face

into its constituent triangles

tears of pain

become indistinguishable

from tears of joy

3.

in the silk-darkened room

you come to me

with the sound of kisses

on your bare feet

they grow more distant

with your every step

II. the obligatory dream

Georg sees Karla walking down the street toward him. He is overjoyed—he has been wanting to see her.

She sees him too for she waves at him and speeds up. He does the same.

The distance between them grows smaller and smaller.

He can see her face. She is smiling. He smiles back and opens his arms in anticipation of embracing her.

She does the same.

He can't wait until they are together.

Only steps separate them. The moment of joy is almost there.

Then suddenly there is emptiness before him. He has passed her. Their bodies have gone through each other like two clouds of vapor.

He turns around in despair, stops, and searches for her with his eyes.

She is walking away but has also turned her head around and is looking at him. She waves in a friendly fashion.

He shouts, Karla stop! Come back!

She yells back, We have merged, Georg! We have merged!

She turns her head away and keeps on walking.

A stab of unbelievable pain pierces his heart.

12. after the funeral

Three days after Karla's funeral Georg was walking down the road through the fields in which he and Karla had spent so many hours together.

As always it was spring and sap in plants shone topaz-like like the evil eyes of a snake. Earthworms were having the time of their lives underground romping around in the soft black earth like miniature whales in water, gobbling it up in great quantities and from time to time sending it skyward in tiny dark geysers. Beetles pushed huge balls of dung carefully like mothers their babies in tall unsteady prams.   The bright green grass squeaked like a rubber duck in water under the pressure of his gaze.

The unpaved road surrounded by big gnarled willow trees resembling old women in the act of mourning curved first this way, then that, and then this way again through the flat landscape like a drunk having a hard time walking in a straight line.   No sooner had the horizon below the sapphire sky gotten nearer than it was far off again at times even farther than before.

Georg walked on.

Eventually he found himself in a strange landscape.   He had never walked this far before.   The ground all around was uneven as if covered with molehills and dark green, almost black.   There were light patches in spots on it however, almost golden, with the vegetation pale at the tips, straining to the utmost to bring some joy into the gloomy landscape.   The ground looked squishy too as if overgrown with water-laden moss.   Here and there dwarf pines grew in clusters like kids gathered in hostile gangs in a schoolyard during a recess.   Georg decided to stop there and explore the surroundings.   He stepped off the road to his right and proceeded walking.

The ground in fact was squishy underfoot and covered with thick water-laden moss as it had looked from the road. Within seconds Georg's shoes became filled with water. It felt cold on his feet like a knife blade looking for the proper spot where to cut. He seemed to be walking on a soft mattress and at times his feet sank into the moss up to his ankles. Water kept creeping up his pants and eventually they became wet all the way up to his knees. Still he pressed on.

The clumps of moss gradually got taller and taller and it was hard walking among them. Georg grew tired and decided to rest. He found a clump almost as tall as a chair and wearily sat down on top of it.

It felt comfortable at first like an armchair but then his seat started getting wet and it was clear things would get worse. He ignored the feeling however as well as the prospect of what was to come, decided to stay where he was, and looked around.

Tiny lakes, sometimes no bigger than a few yards across, dotted the landscape all the way to the horizon like the eyes of thousands upon thousands of people lying flat on their backs staring in a stupor at the sky.

the school

I. arrival

As RR stepped out of his car he was surprised. He had driven up all the time since turning off the main road and expected to find himself on top of a mountain but here he was in the middle of a valley with sizeable peaks all around.

The mountains cradled the landscape below like hands cupped around a precious object or parents fearfully shielding their small child and after the initial disappointment he relaxed. There was something wonderfully peaceful about the spot.

His car stood on his left a few feet away from him and he heard the ticking noises its engine made as it was cooling off. These reminded him of the sounds mice used to make chewing on something inside walls or up in the attic he used to hear lying in his bed at night unable to sleep as a little boy. This in turn brought back to him the feeling of peace and safety of those happy childhood days when he lived with his family in their big house without a care in the world. He felt like that now. He had finally come home after all these years!

Some fifty feet before him stood the building. It was single-storied, low, with a flat roof and a plain façade looking like a store in an unimposing small town commercial street. There was no sign on, next to, or above it explaining its nature which he expected based on the impressive one that made him turn off the main road and make the detour.

In the middle of the façade there was a wide sliding glass door with similar looking wide but much shorter windows symmetrically spaced on both sides of it. Darkness lay behind the former and the latter making it look as if the building was abandoned. This clearly wasn't so judging by the thick layer of gravel covering the parking area in front of the building and even more the immaculately swept and maintained concrete path leading from it to the door.

RR stepped forward, crossed the distance separating him from the path, stepped up onto it, and walked along it to the door which opened by itself when he was a couple of steps away.

2. reception

Inside, the ceiling was low and darkness stretched under it into the depth of the building like a rail track going off into the tunnel in a coal mine. Rows of neon lights were recessed in the ceiling but they were dark and RR concluded there was something wrong with electricity in the building and they had been temporarily turned off. He could see pretty well all around however.

Straight before him barring his way curved a tall roughly four foot high barrier of light laminated wood forming a half-circle. It was the reception desk. In the very middle of it up front stood a tall cylindrical stainless steel vase filled with huge white flowers on massive green stalks, most likely gladioli, its bottom hidden by the edge of the desk sticking up. Behind the desk high up on a freestanding wall covered with gray slate hung a round burnished stainless steel clock with no numbers on its face and its hands missing. There was a small hole in its center with an even smaller rod protruding out of it where the hands were normally attached. Something was obviously wrong with the clock as well perhaps connected with the problem with electricity. Directly above the hole you could make out a small capital Greek letter omega (Ω) traced out in gold—he concluded almost certainly the name of its manufacturer.

Instinctively RR glanced at his watch and noted it showed 4:07. It had taken him nearly an hour to get to the place. It was about quarter after three when he turned off the main road. It had seemed much shorter to him however—more like ten minutes. It was incredible what tricks your mind would sometimes play on you.

He expected to find the figure of the receptionist behind the flower vase but as he stepped to the side and peeked he saw no one. The place wasn't completely dead however—he could hear the soft labial sounds a fountain was making somewhere close by, he guessed most likely behind the wall.

Dark corridors channeling the darkness ran on both sides of the desk with a pale smudge of daylight staining the one on the left some twenty feet ahead.

As RR stood thinking if he should announce his arrival by calling out Hello, the smudge vanished for an instant and when it reappeared he saw the figure of a woman in white walk in a energetic step toward him.

She was of average height and build, had short blond hair, wore big heavy-rimmed glasses, and was dressed in a white coat such as medical personnel wear.

I'm Dr. Erde Mr. Rohark, she said extending her hand for RR to shake while still a couple of steps away. I'm glad to meet you. We've been waiting for you, she added, squeezing his hand which he mechanically stuck out toward her.

It was small but strong and pleasantly warm and dry.

The cold and bony hand of fear reached out from somewhere inside RR and squeezed his heart. How on earth did she know his name? He had decided to come to the place at the moment he was driving past the sign on the main road announcing it and had never talked about it to anyone. In fact he had hardly been aware the place existed, had never thought much about it, and had certainly never planned to visit it. Even now he didn't know why he was there.

His ears seemed to have filled with blood and his heartbeat was deafening.

How do you know my name? He asked feebly barely able to hear himself talk.

Richard Rohark. Isn't it right? She smiled adding his first name to let him know she wasn't mistaking him for someone else. There are ways, she laughed. Extrasensory perception or license plates.... Don't worry, she added. There's nothing magic about it and certainly nothing malicious.

Let's step into my office, she concluded putting her hand on his arm and moving in the direction she came from.

Excuse the fact I am welcoming you myself, she continued as he
was following her. We're momentarily short on help. And excuse
the darkness, she added. There's something wrong with the lights
and they've been working on them since this morning but still
haven't fixed them.

Yes, I thought that was the reason it was so dark here, RR
mumbled barely audibly still not quite recovered from being
unsettled.

Does it have something to do with the clock? He added trying to
mask his feelings. Its hands are missing.

No, the woman laughed softly. That's a separate problem. There
was something wrong with one of the hands and we are expecting
a replacement from the manufacturer. It's been like this for a
couple of weeks. It takes forever for anyone to respond these
days. But it should be here any day. We were told it's been
shipped.

But how come your fountain is working? RR asked genuinely
interested having nearly recovered his composure as they were
stepping into the woman's office. Isn't it run by electricity? Is the
water coming in from the outside?

Oh, the woman said laughing once more as she walked behind the desk, It isn't a fountain. It's a recording.... It's simpler and cheaper that way. And it's only the lights in this part of the building that aren't working. The sound system is fine.

Please have a seat, she concluded sitting down and pointing to the chair across the desk from her as he remained standing.

Do you have trouble hiring people? RR asked sitting down after moving the chair a little to make it easier for himself to do it. He was glad to go on to a new topic having been so wrong in his guesses in connection with the old one. He had assumed the clock was made by the Omega Company but given his track record so far he feared it was not impossible he was wrong on this account too.

The woman said nothing and inexplicably leaned forward over the desk and looked deep into his eyes.

That, yes, she said quietly. But they die too, she added mysteriously in a near whisper.

Once again the hand of fear reached out from deep inside him and grabbed his heart and then he realized for the first time that behind the façade of professionalism the woman was very feminine and exceptionally beautiful, especially her eyes, which were extraordinary—the color of rushing water in a mountain brook.

3. or

Some half a dozen steps led down from the door to the corridor which stretched for what seemed like a good hundred feet straight ahead. It was wide with a gray tiled floor which shone in the strong sunlight coming from the left as if flooded with water. The wall on that side was all floor to ceiling glass divided into partitions some ten feet wide. Beyond it lay the enclosed courtyard garden with big exotic plants—cacti, sisal, henequen, agaves—all fiercely and occasionally successfully imitating the two fountains breaking up into three even segments the wide path that dissected the courtyard in two, and less fiercely and completely unsuccessfully the distant snow-capped mountain peaks protruding above the flat roof of the building on the other side. A long row of doors, too many to count at a glance, punctuated the gray wall on the right.

RR quickly ran down the steps, walked up to the first door, and softly knocked on it. He felt he might as well be methodical and start at the beginning.

There was no answer to his knocking, he knocked again and as there again was no answer he put his hand on the door handle, pushed down on it, and stepped forward. Obediently the door opened letting him in. He closed it shut behind him.

The room was big with a high ceiling, more like a ballroom than a regular room, and empty of furniture and people. Its walls were peach colored and had ornate cornices running along the four sides under the ceiling. Three huge chandeliers like giant swarms of crystal and bright-light bees hanging down from the ceiling illuminated the room revealing all its scanty details—the color of its walls, the floral shapes of the cornices, the sharp lines and corners where the walls met, and the immaculately clean shiny amber parquet floor. The room obviously had recently been attended to.

RR stopped abruptly as soon as he closed the door threatened by the huge space as if by a deep precipice directly before him. An unpleasant feeling which he knew well but momentarily couldn't name welled up inside him making him want to leave the room as soon as possible. It was different from chills running up one's spine in its physical effect but very much like it in the psychological one. Quickly he checked if he missed seeing something or someone in the room but there was definitely nothing and no one there and he sharply turned around, opened the door, and stepped back into the corridor once again shutting the door behind him. As he was stepping out he instinctively looked for a light switch next to the door to turn out the lights but there was none and he resigned himself to leaving the emptiness behind him clear for anyone to see.

Instinctively following his decision to be methodical he walked up to the next door, knocked on it, and this time without waiting for an answer opened it and stepped inside closing the door shut once again.

The room was much smaller than the first one, both narrower and shorter, and for some reason with a much lower ceiling. It was dark with green walls but had a cluster of bright electric lights shining down from the ceiling onto what appeared to be a table or a stand in the center. A sizeable group of people, roughly a dozen, clustered around this table/stand, apparently watching what was going on there. They were all dressed in green gowns and had caps of the same color on their heads. It looked like he was in an operating room. An operation seemed to be in progress with students watching.

Embarrassed RR was about to turn around and once more walk out but at that instant one of the people in the group turned around and motioned for him to come forward. From the rounded squat shape of the figure and even more from its broad soft-featured face RR concluded it was a woman.

She smiled broadly at RR and once more vigorously motioned for him to come forward. She then moved over and made room on her right for him to step into.

Emboldened RR walked up to the woman and stood beside her. She greeted him with what sounded like a soft sigh, moved over a little more to the left to make more room for him, and turned forward to watch the action going on in the center as she had been doing before. She had to crane her neck to do this. RR made himself more comfortable in the wider space and peeked over the shoulder of the person in front of him. He was the taller of the two and had no trouble seeing what was happening.

There indeed was a tall table in the center with someone lying face up on it and two men dressed like the rest of the people were busy doing something to him/her. The person's dark green gown had been pulled all the way up to the chin having bunched up there so that the face was not visible but the body from the top of the chest to the feet was naked. From its whiteness, frailty, and rounded forms RR once again concluded it was a woman. Strange as it seemed she was apparently undergoing an operation without being covered up as patients invariably are on such occasions nowadays.

Having concluded the person was a woman RR noticed the other obvious female features he had missed at the beginning—the round bulging breasts as if apples had been inserted under her skin over the pectoral muscles, the complete absence of body hair, the translucency and milkiness of the skin, and the delicate pubis unmarred by the male organ. The hair over it must have been recently trimmed because the skin under it was visible and it looked more like a shadow being cast over the spot than hair growing on it. It reminded RR of dusk.

RR was ready to grow sexually excited by what he saw but remembered the nature of the situation and his feeling dissipated quickly like steam in the air.

He concentrated on what the two men were doing to the woman and to his surprise saw that they didn't have scalpels in their hands but felt-tipped pens and were tracing out various patterns on the woman's abdomen in black ink. Some of these were drawn in solid lines, other in dotted ones, some of the latter dense, other spaced far apart. They looked strange on the pristine skin, on the one hand ugly because of marring its whiteness but on the other one beautiful because of their strangeness.

What was going on? RR thought. Are the men making markings where to cut or are they doing something else?

He concluded these couldn't be markings for incisions because there were too many of them.

So what else could they be? He wondered. A thought crossed his mind that this wasn't an operating room but an art class—the men weren't doctors but artists who were showing the students how to do design on the human body.

But why then was everyone wearing green gowns and caps like medical personnel do? He further wondered. It didn't make sense.

Just then one of the men produced from somewhere a big red marker and proceeded to write with it over the woman's body in the lower right part of the abdomen. He was running the marker back and forth in one spot leaving an ugly mark as if trying to cover up something under it. In addition to looking ugly the mark looked terrifying—like blood running out of a wound on the woman's belly.

This should have added to RR's theory the men were doing body art work but something about the brutality of the red color and the ugliness of the mark made him reject it. He didn't know what the process going on meant but was sure it was nothing pleasant.

Just at that instant again a couple of men separated themselves from the group of onlookers. They stepped up to the table and, one of them lifting the woman by her shoulders and the other one by her feet, lifted her up and as the people parted to let them pass carried her toward a door in the far left corner of the room. It was only then RR noticed it was there.

There was total darkness behind the door and they vanished in it.

The woman had hung limply, her body sagging in the middle but from the way her arms swung it didn't look as though she was unconscious.

When the door shut one of the men who had worked on the woman turned to the crowd and asked loudly, Who wants to be next?

RR's heart beat faster and for an instant he couldn't catch his breath. He didn't know why this was happening but felt a premonition he might be involved in what was to come.

Nobody? The man asked smiling. You're afraid? There's no need to be. It doesn't hurt.

Come on! He urged the people before him. One of you.... Come on!

He'll go next, he heard the woman who had invited him in speak up grabbing his left arm and trying to push him forward.

What? RR shouted trying to keep his voice low. Me? Why?... What is it?

It's just a training run for the operation, the woman whispered. They check different parts of the body and finally decide where the trouble might lie.... Where the person might be operated on eventually.

Go on! She spoke up loudly. Go!

He's coming, she shouted toward the man by the table. He's just scared.

No need to be, the man said reassuringly. It won't hurt. Come on!

Go ahead! Go! The woman shouted pushing RR forward.

She held him fast by his arm and wouldn't let go as he tried to free himself.

No! RR bellowed in a desperate voice. I don't want to go! I just peeked in here. I don't have to participate.

Go! Go! The woman yelled, her fingers sunk into his flesh like teeth, trying to push him forward. Her face was a broad white stain in the half darkness with the two bulging eyes and the frightening gaping dark hole of her mouth in the center.

RR tried to free himself with still move vigor but felt someone's very strong hands grab his right arm and push him likewise forward. It was the man on his right. He had a bony face and was at least as tall as he and very strong.

Go ahead! Go! The man shouted accompanying the woman's cries.

Let me go! RR roared and mustering all his strength tore himself free from the hands of the two people.

Having freed himself he ran as fast as he could to the door he had come in through, opened it, quickly stepped out into the corridor, and shut the door with a bang behind him.

Once there he stopped however and stood panting looking to his right and left not knowing which way to go.

4. stretching

A room looking like a car garage. Concrete floor, bare wood walls with big nails driven into them, various kinds of tools and utensils suspended on the latter, for instance hammers, hacksaws, wrenches, pliers, gardening shears, spades, hoes, rakes. All sort of junk also on the floor, especially in the corners—an old lawn mower, a rusty wheel barrow, a rusty and dusty kerosene stove, and so forth. A small square window high up in one of the walls, a mountainous landscape outside it blurred by a thick layer of yellow dust with the outline of a mountain range shining through it like a graph describing a gradual impressive growth of a company ending in an abrupt near absolute collapse.

Five persons—four students and a facilitator—gathered in a circle in the center of the room. The students—Kristina, Sophie, Walter, and RR. The facilitator—another man named Walter.

Kristina in her mid fifties, heavyset, dumpy, with greasy gray hair
bunched up carelessly in the back of her head and a fat pasty face
with sharp lines going down from the sides of her mouth to her
chin making her look like an antique talking doll. Dressed in a
gray long-sleeved shirt and a long black skirt that trails on the
floor up front.

Sophie about sixteen, slight but with soft feminine forms, dark
curly hair neatly combed back and carefully tied into a pony tail in
the back, a pale face slightly puffy as if from recent crying, a
delicate mouth swollen on one side as if from a passionate love
bite, and big iris-blue eyes. Dressed in a dark flowery dress more
fit for an older woman than for a girl her age and a pale blue
sweater open down the middle fit even more for an older woman
than for a girl her age.

Walter the student in his early sixties, tall, bony, with a matching
bony face and thick salt and pepper hair sticking high up front.
Wears a red and black lumber jacket and a pair of jeans that have
lost their color and taken on the shape of his bony lower body.

Walter the facilitator in his late twenties, thin, of above average
height, with a boyish face and dark hair starting to turn thin on
top.   Dressed in a slightly worn dark blue business suit, a

somewhat rumpled white shirt, and a limp blue and red striped tie.

The group is learning the technique of stretching. Kristina has volunteered to be the first to try.

Walter the facilitator *(to Kristina)*: Are you ready now Kristina?

Kristina *(laconically)*: Yes.

Walter the facilitator *(opens the folder and leafs through the pages in it while speaking)*: I have some examples here for you to help you learn this technique. *(To the other students.)* You guys study these carefully too because I don't want to have to go through them for each of you separately. You'll remember what I say and try to learn from what Kristina does too. *(Continues speaking to everybody.)* We thought having examples from the field of art... ancient masters... would be better than real life examples... photographs. They give you not only the physical characteristics but also the emotions behind them which is just as important for achieving the result. *(After a pause.)* Unfortunately I wasn't able to find that much. But I do have a couple of things. *(Takes out a page with a picture on it looking like a photograph of a pale beige clay tile.)* Here is a picture of a carving... a relief... of the martyrdom of St. John Sarkander. He's a Polish and Czech priest from the seventeenth century who died on a rack... was tortured for not divulging what he'd been told in a confession. It's from his gravestone. See how his feet are fastened on one end and hands tied to the rope that is attached to the wheel? When the wheel is turned it stretches the body. (*He opens the folder wide and sticks out his hand forward for everyone to see. Shows with his finger what he is referring to. The students cluster around him and face the same way as he to see better.*) He's vertical here... standing up... but usually the victim was laid down horizontally on rollers so that his body would slide better. (*After a pause.*) See how obedient he is?... How he's letting his body obey the force of the pulling? You should do the same listening to your inner voice. (*Puts the picture under the other ones in the folder and pulls out another one. It is colorful in comparison with the preceding one, full of black, white, brown, blue, and red.*) And here's a reproduction of the painting of the martyrdom of St. Philip by the Spanish painter José de Ribera. (*Lets the students study the picture.*) He was crucified but the painting shows him being lifted up on the cross by ropes. See how his upper body is stretched out?... It's disproportionately long in comparison with the lower half... down below his waist. (*After a pause.*) Look at those arms... how long they are.... How their muscles are yielding to the force of the pull. And how white the upper body is... the chest. (*As an aside.*) Try to remember this. You'll need it for one of the later lessons. (*The students study the picture carefully. He puts it away and takes out another one. It is a* reproduction of an etching showing a woman suspended on a rope by her arms with a heavy weight attached to her feet.) And here's another way of stretching. It was a popular practice in Russia. They would tie a big log to the feet and then lift the person up on a rope. Here it's a stone or an iron weight and it's a woman. It's probably from England and not from Russia. I remember seeing one from Russia with a man and a huge log. It was wonderful but I couldn't find it. (After a pause.) But this one will do. (After a longer pause.) See how obedient she is? How she lets the weight stretch her body out making the muscles vertical... parallel to the force of the pull.... No resistance at all. This insures maximum extension... perfection.... Now you should try to achieve this on your own. It's difficult... in some sense more difficult than what I've shown you.... But you'll have to learn to achieve it. (Closing the folder and turning to Kristina.) Now Kristina, you go ahead and try. (Kristina doesn't move, not knowing how to proceed. He takes charge. Speaks to the other students.) Step aside now and let Kristina lie down on the floor. (The other students step aside and form a circle. He takes Kristina by the arm and stands her in the center of the circle the other students have formed. Speaks to her.) Lie down Kristina, lie down. (Kristina lies down on her back, her figure a big bump on the flat floor. He speaks to her again.) This won't do Kristina, this won't do. You're too bulky. You're a bump. You're supposed to stretch out and be as flat as possible... as close to the ground as you can... ideally merged with it.... You won't achieve it but you should try. (*After a pause.*) Now go ahead and try.

Kristina stirs and apparently makes an inner effort to stretch out but there is little visible result. She is still a bulky mound, a huge bump on the perfectly flat surface of the concrete floor.

Walter the facilitator (*not satisfied*): It's not good enough Kristina, not good enough. Try some more. (*To the other students.*) You guys go ahead and help her. Urge her on.

Walter the student bends down and tries to pull on Kristina's feet. Walter the facilitator is visibly incensed.

Walter the facilitator (*aghast*): No! No hands! (*Walter the student shoots up and steps back embarrassed.*) No physical helping! No hands you guys! Just verbal help... encouragement... she has to do it on her own. (*After a pause, to everyone, gesticulating with his hands.*) Come on Kristina! Stretch, stretch, stretch!

The other three students (*loudly, their faces turning red*): Come on Kristina! Stretch, stretch, stretch!

Kristina wiggles on the floor like a giant stubby worm.

Walter the facilitator (first to Kristina and then to the other three students): Come on Kristina! Stretch, stretch, stretch!

The other three students (shouting, their faces beet-red): Come on Kristina! Stretch, stretch, stretch!

They repeat this a few times with Walter the facilitator having joined in. Kristina continues wiggling desperately on the floor. The process is then repeated over and over with some of the people from time to time bending down in the knees and gesticulating with their clenched fists, and with time amazingly the mound gets lower and longer. Against all odds Kristina is stretching out. The four people keep on urging her and Kristina keeps getting thinner and longer. Joy can be seen shining through on everyone's faces.

5. measurements

There is a knock on the door and before RR has time to say, Come in, it opens and a nondescript blond girl dressed in white steps in.

He thinks it is one of the cleaning ladies but she has a clipboard and a pen in her hand and he concludes it is one of the attendants.

RR stirs annoyed in his bed turning toward her and she comes up to it and says, I have come to take your measurements.

My measurements? RR asks surprised and still more annoyed. Measurements for what?

For whatever might be needed, the girl replies.

Like a suit? RR says, now only puzzled.

Yes, like a suit, but other things too, the girl says, obviously anxious to get the introductory part over and get down to business. We always take measurements of everyone here.

She probably has a busy schedule ahead.

RR decides to stop arguing and says, Do I have to get up or will you do it with me lying down?

No, you have to get up, the girl answers. I can't do it with you lying down.

Once more annoyed RR lets out a long loud sigh through his nose, throws back the cover, and starts getting up.

I have nothing under the nightshirt, he says to the girl as a warning.

It's up to you, she replies. You can put something on if you'll be more comfortable that way.

I'll be alright, RR says his feet already on the floor. I was worrying about you.

The girl doesn't reply to his remark but watches him stand up. A tape measure has appeared from nowhere in her hand.

Do you want to put on your slippers? She asks.

I'll be fine this way, he says. Let's get going.

Alright, the girl says. The first measurement we take is your shoulders. Turn around please.

The girl puts the clipboard and pen on the bedside table, RR turns around, she reaches up to his shoulders, and measures them.

Fifty-four centimeters, she says, turns around, writes the number down on the clipboard with the pen, and says, You have broad shoulders.

I do? RR says, and then adds, I guess I do. I must have known it but have forgotten.

He wants to turn around but the girl says, Stay there. We'll measure next the length from the middle of your back to your wrist.

Stick out your left arm, she says as she comes up to him.

So it's for a suit, RR says doing what the girl has asked him.

It could be, the girl replies laconically and performs the measurement.

Seventy-eight centimeters, she informs RR and records the figure on the clipboard.

The number means nothing to RR and he stays silent.

Turn around now please, the girl says. We'll measure your chest.

RR turns around and automatically spreads his arms out so as to be measured.

The girl performs the measurement and says, One meter thirteen.

Is it good? RR asks.

It's not bad, the girl replies once again laconically writing down the measurement.

RR is a shade disappointed but doesn't know what to say and stays silent.

I will measure your waist now, the girl says stepping up to RR.

RR automatically sucks in his stomach and sticks his arms out to the sides to make it easier for the girl to do her job.

She quickly performs the measurement. The tape measure is loose around RR's waist.

The tape was loose around my waist, RR says.

It's alright, the girl says. This'll make it possible for you to gain weight.

I won't gain any weight here, RR says.

The girl ignores RR's comment and writes the figure down on the clipboard.

It's seventy-two centimeters, she says. Your waist is like a girl's. It's not much bigger than mine.

How much is yours? RR asks.

Sixty-eight, the girl replies. I've gained weight.

Are you pregnant? RR asks.

Not yet, the girl replies.

RR wants to pursue the subject but the girl is clearly anxious to do her work and so he says nothing.

Now we'll measure your seat, the girl says bending down and putting the tape measure around RR's pelvis.

You mean my bottom? RR asks.

Seat or bottom it's the same, the girl replies and performs the measurement.

Seventy-eight centimeters, she says as she turns around to write the figure down.

How is it? RR asks. Good or bad?

It's not bad for a man, the girl replies.

RR entertains the notion of asking her dimension in this area but decides not to. He suddenly feels bored.

Now we will measure waist to ankle, the girl says and proceeds to perform the measurement.

When she doesn't tell RR how much it was he feels concerned.

How much is it? He asks.

One meter exactly, the girl replies.

The number once again means nothing to RR and so he remains quiet feeling sulky.

Next we'll do the inseam, the girl says. From your crotch to your ankle.

My crotch? RR asks concerned. I have nothing underneath.

We will do it through the nightshirt, the girl says.

Here take the end and put it inside your crotch and I will go down to the ankle, she adds.

RR presses the end of the tape measure up front in his pubic area.

The girl watches and corrects him.

No, no, she says. Inside your crotch, between the legs, where they meet, next to the scrotum.

A streak of malice wells up inside RR. He would really like to finally give it to the girl.

I can't do it through the shirt, he says through his teeth. It'll change the measurement. I'll do it *au naturelle* if you don't mind.

He is afraid what he is planning to do might be too daring and decides to warn the girl.

I'll have to lift the shirt, he says.

The girl says nothing as she is looking down on the floor fiddling around his ankle and RR decides to go through with his plan.

He lifts his shirt and presses the end of the tape as the girl told him.

I have it in place, he says still clenching his teeth.

The girl glances up, his penis sways back and forth in front of her nose like a fly trying to land there, but she says nothing. She lowers her head and proceeds to read the measurement.

RR looks down at her and sees his penis hover over her head limp and useless like a bell clapper with no bell around it.

The girl totally disregards the situation. She is probably used to this kind of harassment and has found an effective way of dealing with it.

Seventy-eight, she says standing up as if nothing had happened. She pulls the tape measure out of RR's hand and goes over to the bedside table to write the figure down.

RR lets the hem of his shirt drop. He is totally deflated at not having unsettled the girl and the number once more means nothing to him so he stays silent. He is tired of the whole procedure and would like it to end as soon as possible. He assumes it is over.

It doesn't appear to be however. The girl comes up to him with the tape measure in her hand and says, We have one more measurement to do... your height.

It's one meter eighty-six, RR says quickly.

We have to measure it, the girl says. People's height changes... gets smaller as they get older.

But why do you need it? RR asks suddenly worried. You don't need it for a suit.

We always take it, the girl replies. It could be needed.

For what? RR asks fear rising up in him and his heart starting to pound.

Whatever, the girl replies evasively and drops the subject. Here, take it and press it to the top of your head... here, she says and presses the tape measure to RR's forehead so that part of it sticks up apparently to the level of the crown of his head.

RR wants to argue with the girl but gives up. He knows in the end she will win out so he does as he is told.

The girl bends down to the floor and performs the measurement.

One meter eighty-four, she says standing up and writes the figure on the clipboard.

I guess I shrunk by two centimeters, RR says feebly and the girl replies quietly as if to herself, Two centimeters isn't bad.

She writes something else on the clipboard, says, We're all done now. Good-bye, and walks out of the room before RR has time to say anything.

He stands in an uncomfortable position looking at the door as at a train he has just missed.

6. stilling

The same garage-like room. Walter the student stretched out on his back on the floor in the middle of the room with the other three students and Walter the facilitator around him. The latter on Walter the student's left bent over him, watching him closely, the manila folder in his left hand pressed to his chest, the striped tie helplessly hanging down. The group is learning the technique of being still. The lesson has been going on for a while.

Walter the facilitator: You're doing great Walter. No wonder your middle name is Peter. You're still as a rock. (*Changing the tone of his voice.*) But be careful with your breathing. Your chest has just moved up and down.

Walter the student (*visibly trying to stay still while moving his lips*): I couldn't help it. I had to breathe.

Walter the facilitator: Breathing is fine for now. We'll come to stopping it later. But you must breathe in such a way that your chest doesn't heave. Do it by moving your diaphragm up and down without expanding your ribcage. (*Pauses while watching Walter the student carefully. Not sure what is going on.*) Are you breathing now?

Walter the student (*perfectly still, practically not moving his lips*): Yes.
I can do it fine without moving my chest.

Walter the facilitator (*straightening up, pleased*):   That's great.
You're really like a rock Peter.   (*Catches his mistake.*)   I mean
Walter.   (*Notices a slight movement in one of Walter the student's feet.*)
But keep your feet still.   No movement whatsoever.   You've lain
still now for only a couple of minutes but you know how long
you'll have to lie without moving during the final exam.... So you
mustn't move even the tiniest bit.   Still as a rock! (*Watches Walter
the student carefully.   Is pleased by what he sees.*)

There is total silence in the room with the three students and
Walter the facilitator watching Walter the student lying stretched
out on the floor.   He is absolutely still will no sign of life in him.

Walter the facilitator (*after a couple of minutes' pause*): You're doing
really great Walter but remember there may be distractions.
There could be flies crawling over your face and hands and worms
working your way into your body... even rats chewing at your
fingers and toes.... And you still have to lie still.   Could you do it?

Walter the student (*perfectly still without the slightest sign of movement
of his lips*): Yes.

Walter the facilitator: Great. (*Turing to the other three students.*) Now you guys will have to provide the distraction. (*To Kristina.*) You Kristina will be a fly... flies. You'll gently run your hands and fingers over Walter's face. (*To Sophie.*) And you Sophie will be worms... a worm... trying to squeeze its way into Walter's flesh. (*Turning to RR.*) And you RR will be a rat. You'll chew on his fingers and toes.

RR (*surprised, even distraught*): Chew on them?

Walter the facilitator (*quickly*): With your fingers... pinching... imitating chewing. I didn't mean it literally. (*After a pause, when RR remains silent.*) Is that fine?

RR (*hesitating, uncertain*): Yes,... I guess. (*After a pause.*) But how will I get to his toes? He's wearing shoes.

Walter the facilitator: You can leave out the toes for now.... Work on his legs... through his pants... imitating nibbling. (*After a pause, when RR doesn't respond. Being conciliatory.*) All right. I will be a rat too and will take care of his legs. You work on his fingers. (*After a brief pause.*) Alright?

RR (*not enthusiastic but agreeing*): Alright.

Walter the facilitator: But you and Kristina will have to be careful so as not to interfere with each other. *(Remembers RR's objection. To Sophie.)* And you Sophie you don't have to get under his clothes to try getting into his body. Do it through his clothes... with your fingers.

Sophie *(calmly)*: Yes of course. I understood that.

Walter the facilitator *(satisfied)*: Good. *(After a pause.)* Alright now. We all get down on our knees and do what we're supposed to. *(Without a pause.)* Come on.

He moves toward Walter the student's feet and gets down on his knees. The other three students kneel down too—Kristina and Sophie on Walter the student's right, the former near his face and the latter lower down, and RR on Walter the student's left, near his chest.

Everyone immediately starts performing the assigned task— Kristina runs the tips of her fingers over Walter the student's face, Sophie bores with one of her fingers into Walter the student's chest, RR pinches the latter's fingers with his own, and Walter the facilitator does the same with the man's calves through his pants.

The exercise goes on. The four distracters vary what they do but Walter the student lies still as a rock with no sign of life in him.

7. erta

It must have gotten much warmer during the night because water was dripping off the icicles hanging down from the eaves outside the window each drop magnifying the world behind it as it fell through the air as if in order to reveal to him some essential truth about it which was not visible to the naked eye. There wasn't enough time for him to grasp it however. The drops appeared to fall exactly at the rate of one per second.

It was late in the morning, much later than when he usually woke up, and sunshine was impatiently forcing its way into the room through the floor to ceiling window. The radiators were going full blast however and the air was stifling hot and dry. To be more comfortable he had pushed the blanket off himself in his sleep.

Instinctively he turned his head left to see if she had done the same but she was covered all the way up to the top of her head with her part of it. Only her hair was left visible on the pillow like golden wheat kernels gathered in a compact mound. She lay on her left side curled up with her back to him.

Without planning to do it he raised himself up on his left elbow and touched her shoulder gently with the fingers of his right hand.

Immediately she rolled over on her back and turning her head further to the right looked at him and smiled warmly. She hadn't been asleep.

He leaned over to kiss her and found himself on top of her. Their mouths joined and he was surprised he was so ready. She opened to him naturally like tall grass parting and as twice during the night he relived that softness and warmth he had always suspected was part of life but which he was experiencing only for the first time now. The memories of all the pains and sufferings he had lived through no longer mattered. They were like a child's toys. It had been silly of him to hang on to them.

From close up her eyes were even more amazing. Beautifully rounded pebbles were magnified on their bottom and tiny fishes trembled in their crystalline water.

What's your name? He asked as his breathing came back to normal and he lay stretched out next to her.

I mean your first name, he added hastily.

Erta, she replied softly.

Erta Erde, he said with a note of humor in his voice. Did your parents choose Erta to go with your last name so you'd have EE for initials?

No, she said smiling. (He could tell she did this from the tone of her voice.) I changed my name myself. It was Herta and I dropped the H. But then I dropped the initial H in my last name too... as well as the final r. Our surname was... is... Herder. I was called Herta Herder. But my parents did name me Herta to go with Herder. All three of us were HH – Heinrich Herder my father, Hilde Herder my mother, and Herta Herder me.

But why did you do it? He asked. Because of what the word means?

That was part of it, she said. But I was young and rebellious.... Wanted to break away from my parents' authority.... But I wasn't able to do it completely, she added laughing softly. I was left with EE which copies HH. I didn't realize it at the time but it was in obedience to my parents. You can't escape those things.

RR and EE, he said quietly, then added enthusiastically, ErEr and ErEr, and stopped abruptly, not knowing how to continue.

Yes, she said. I noticed it when you came. Did your parents do it on purpose? ... Were their initials also RR?

No, he replied. My father's name was Arnold and my mother's Maria. And my brother's name is Walter. It was just a coincidence. But kids in school started calling me RR and it stuck. That's all.

They lay silent, their bodies touching, her much warmer than his as he could tell from the way it felt hot to him. They had exhausted all they had to say.

Then he felt her stir and looked left.

She was raising herself up.

Do you have to go now? He asked aware the question was superfluous.

Yes, she said as she sat up and stayed there momentarily before proceeding. It's late. They're waiting for me.... I'm never this late.

Yes, he said planning to go on but then ran out of words. He didn't try searching for new ones knowing there weren't any.

She dressed as naturally as she had made love and he watched her attentively as something interesting going on in a movie on a screen.

When she was finished she came back to the bed, leaned over it, kissed him on the mouth, said, You can cry now, and walked out of the room.

Outside, the corridor was bright as if with sunlight. You could hear the sound of distant voices.

He stretched out on his back again, closed his eyes, and covered his face with his hands pressing them tightly together in the middle and letting them go down at an angle along the sides of his face like a book.

8. closing

A small white room with two sloping walls and sheer white curtains on the two recessed windows in one of the sloping walls looking like a child's attic bedroom. An enameled white bed with a big soft pillow and a likewise soft white comforter over it, its head against one of the vertical walls. Sophie stretched out on her back on top of it, arms and legs straight and eyes closed, with the three other students and Walter the facilitator around her— Kristina and RR on the left and the two Walters on the right. Sophie is learning the technique of closing her eyes. The session has just started. (There is no manila folder in Walter the facilitator's hand this time.)

Walter the facilitator (to the three students standing up): Alright you guys, start humming now. Remember, you should sound like a lullaby and music of the spheres at the same time.

The three start humming. The sound goes something like, OOooOOooOOoo, and continues uninterrupted.

Walter the facilitator (to Sophie): Concentrate now Sophie. Eyelids parallel to your arms and legs, parallel to lines going off into infinity... into infinity.... You seeing blackness, blackness. blackness....

The humming goes on and on, OOooOOooOOooOOooOOooO Ooo....

Sophie lies still.

Walter the facilitator *(anxious, to Sophie)*: What do you see?

Sophie *(after a few seconds, in an ethereal voice)*: Stars... beautiful stars... passing by like lights on a night train....

Walter the facilitator *(upset)*: No, Sophie, no! You must see nothing.... Just blackness... total blackness... no lights... nothing... nothing.

Sophie lies still but you can see strain on her face. This goes on for some ten seconds.

Sophie *(finally, with distress in her voice)*: I can't.... I keep seeing these lights... stars.... They're beautiful.

Walter the facilitator *(to those standing up)*: Alright you guys.... Less music.... Just a steady hum.... A monotonous drone... unpleasant.

The hum changes to something like, OOOOOOOOOO....

Walter the facilitator *(to Sophie)*: So concentrate now Sophie. No lights... stars... just blackness... nothing... nothing... black nothing.

Sophie lies as before, the strain on her face becoming more pronounced with time. It looks like she will break out in a sweat any instant.

Then suddenly she gives out an ear-piercing scream, sits up bolt upright, and speaks.

Sophie (*panting heavily, with an expression of terror on her face*): I saw it. It's horrible!

The three other students exchange silent glances. Walter the facilitator looks concerned.

9. sobbing fountains

RR's dream.

It is night. The sky is clear and full of stars. It is vast, stretching as far as the eye can see in all directions. The vista is breathtaking. There is no moon but the stars cast enough light so that it is bright enough to see.

RR is in the courtyard garden. He has come out of his room through the sliding door and is walking down one of the garden paths toward its center. He is barefoot so his feet make no sound as they tread on the graveled path. He is like a cat on the prowl slinking through the night.

He has been looking at the sky and his chest is bursting with joy— he has never seen anything so beautiful before. Everything around him is beautiful too. The plants on both sides and up ahead are huge and look subtropical—nothing but cacti, sisal, henequen, agaves, palm trees, and the like. The air is warm too. It is as if he were finding himself in some warm country like Mexico rather than where he is in reality.

He is moving forward and expects more beautiful things up ahead.

He then remembers the two fountains and the noise they make. He likes it and would like to hear it.

He stops and listens but hears nothing except a faint chirping of crickets on the ground which he hadn't noticed before. He is surprised because the fountains are quite loud but as he listens even more carefully he still cannot hear them.

Concerned he walks more quickly forward, stops, and listens once again. Now he does hear something—faint splashing of water coming from both sides of the garden. (He is walking along a path cutting the garden in two perpendiculars to the one the fountains stand on.) He concludes then the fountains have been turned down for the night to save energy. There is no point pumping water in them full force when there is no one around.

He wants to see what the fountains look like working in this mode and starts up at a faster pace down the path. But then to his surprise he sees another fountain at the intersection of the path he is walking along and the one the fountains are on. It is very strange. There was never one there before. It must have been built recently and he merely hadn't noticed it.

He speeds up so as to get to the fountain as soon as possible. He is very anxious to see it.

He comes to within some ten paces away from it when he realizes the fountain doesn't look like fountains normally do. It is in the shape of a woman standing with her arms hanging down and her face turned up. Her back is turned to him.

He is intrigued by what he sees even more and keeps on walking but then notices the figure moves—it has raised its right arm and brought its hand to its face. The figure isn't a fountain but a living person—a woman.

He freezes instantly breathing heavily and his heart pounding loudly and stands still not knowing what to do.

Instinctively he stifles his breath and hears the woman make the same kind of sound he heard the fountains make. He is puzzled. What is she trying to do? Imitate a fountain?

But then he sees the woman move her arm as if wiping her face with her hand and hears her make a sound such as one makes clearing one's nose and realizes she is not imitating a fountain but crying. She has come out into the garden to be alone and cry so that no one would hear her.

And then to his surprise from the way the woman had moved and from the outline of her body on the slightly lighter background he realizes the woman is Erta.

Overjoyed he plans to run up to her to let her know he has come but stops himself instantly as if about to do something bad. She must not be disturbed. The very thought of doing it makes him feel ashamed.

He stands a few more seconds watching her with a feeling of deep love in his heart and then turns around and as quietly as he can tiptoes down the path in the direction he came from.

10. paling

This time it is a room in what appears to be a flour mill or a bakery. Likewise bare wooden walls but with no nails in them. A broad-planked wooden floor. Sacks full of flour against the walls especially in the corners but otherwise the room empty. Heavy traces of flour on the walls and the floor. A big square window in one of the walls its glass opaque from flour. A mountainous landscape as if in a heavy snowstorm barely shining through it. No graph line of any kind visible this time.

Sophie, Walter the student, RR, and the new facilitator Kristina gathered in a circle in the middle of the room with Kristina the student in the center likewise standing up. Kristina the facilitator is substituting for Walter the facilitator who is indisposed and Kristina the student has again volunteered to be the first to try mastering the technique of turning pale.

Kristina the facilitator a slight but very energetic blonde in her mid twenties dressed in a loose gray sweatshirt and matching baggy pants. Worn, once white tennis shoes on her feet. Thin, nearly white flaxen hair carelessly combed and tied in two scrawny rat-tail braids. Narrow blue eyes. Delicate but elongated nose and lower part of the face. Small white teeth, sharp as if filed down. A shrill voice.

Kristina the facilitator *(to Kristina the student)*: Now Kristina I want you to imagine you are these walls around you and that the flour has settled down on your face... your whole body.

Kristina the student *(puzzled)*: My clothes too?

Kristina the facilitator *(sarcastic)*: What do you think you are? A dry cleaner? You can't make your clothes grow white by merely willing them.... No just your body... your face and the rest of it. *(After a pause.)* But we will see just your face and hands. We can't see through your clothes and you wouldn't want us to peek under them... especially Walter here and RR.... Now would you?

Kristina the student *(serious and obedient)*: No.

Kristina the facilitator: Alright then. Start now. Start turning white.

Kristina the student tries and starts turning red.

Kristina the facilitator sees it instantly and explodes.

Kristina the facilitator *(red in the face herself, at the top of her voice)*:
No, no, no! Don't strain! I told you not to strain. Relax and
think you're those walls... that that flour has settled down on you.
*(After a pause, having watched Kristina the student stop turning red but
not make any progress in the direction if paling.)* That won't do.
You'd better lie down. I know the floor is cold but that'll help
you grow paler. It's hard to do it standing up. *(Takes Kristina the
student by her arm and makes her stretch out on her back on the floor.
Speaks in a more friendly voice.)* Try now. Relax and think of the
flour on the walls.... Turn white, white, white.

Kristina the student lies still but there is no noticeable change in
the color of her face and hands in the white direction. Kristina
the facilitator watches her attentively and then speaks.

Kristina the facilitator: You're not doing it right Kristina. You're
not relaxing. *(After a pause.)* Relax completely and think of
flour... snow... You're looking down a bottomless precipice into
which you might fall... into which you're falling.... You're falling
already.... You're going to get killed... smashed to a bloody pulp
at the bottom.... You're turning white with fear... and cold....
The color of the flour on the walls.... White, white, white.

Walter the student murmurs something. He seems to have noticed a change in Kristina the student's color in the right direction. Kristina the facilitator notices it and is angered.

Kristina the facilitator (*to those standing up*): Keep quiet now guys, keep quiet. Don't disturb Kristina. She needs your help.

Walter the student (*apologetically*): She's started to turn white so I want to encourage her.

Kristina the student (*from down below*): I'm cold.

Kristina the facilitator (*angry with the two*): Quiet now you two. (*To Walter the student.*) You Walter keep your observations to yourself. We see very well what's happening. You don't have to tell us. (*To Kristina the student.*) And you Kristina, no speaking. Just relaxing and turning white. Do you hear me? White, white, white.

There appears to be some progress in the right direction on Kristina the student's part and the students have noticed it. They are keeping quiet watching what Kristina the student is doing as if spellbound. The task is obviously difficult and they are not sure they will be able to perform it as well. Everyone is anxious.

Kristina the facilitator has also noticed Kristina the student's progress and is somewhat pleased with it. She is concerned however there may be problems ahead and tries to prevent them.

Kristina the facilitator (*for the first time calmly and kindly*): You're doing fine now Kristina. You'Sre doing fine. But remember further along you're supposed to start adding some gray. Think about those walls under the flour. They're gray. You're supposed to be like that... gray with white over it.... White on the outside but gray underneath... White and gray, white and gray.

There is deeper concern on the faces of the three students. The task is turning out to be harder than they expected.

II. dr. erde

Breathe deep now, she said pressing the stethoscope to his back.

RR did as he was told and held his breath.

No Mr. Rohark, she corrected him. Don't stop breathing. Long deep breaths. In and out, in and out.

He did as he was told feeling the hard round shape traveling back and forth over his curved back like a drop of water rejoicing at having freed itself from the force of gravity.

The distant mountain peaks looked small peeking over the roof of the building on the other side of the courtyard like kids curious to see what was going on. They seemed to be interested in his fate.

The icicles were still there hanging down from the eaves longer than ever in spite of dripping water day after day. It was the nights that were cold. Winter just didn't want to go away.

Now breathe in deep and hold your breath, she said and he understood what she meant and obeyed her this time.

She listened for a long time, moved the stethoscope to another spot on his back, and pressed it there.

He anticipated what she would say and in advance breathed in deeply and held his breath.

She obviously noticed what he had done and didn't repeat her instruction but also didn't comment on his cooperation but listened attentively for a few seconds and moved the stethoscope to still another spot.

This went on for another half a dozen times or so and then she said, Lie down now please.

He stretched out on his back, she peeled back the covers to below his knees exposing his nakedness, and proceeded to apply the stethoscope to his chest and abdomen telling him to either breathe or not at the proper times.

He thought of a stone being turned over in someone's fingers while studied with interest.

When she had finished she picked up his shirt which she had put on the chair next to the bed after he had given it to her and said, You can put it on now.

He sat up and did as he was told and when he was finished she was already by the door ready to open it.

Once more fear like a strong bony hand grabbed his heart and with his clenched throat in a changed voice he called out, Dr. Erde....

She stopped, turned around, and looking through the heavy glasses with her mountain brook eyes said, Yes?

He seemed only to see the latter.

Nothing, nothing, he said turning red with embarrassment and lay down.

Silently she turned around and walked out of the room.

12. stopping

RR's dream.

RR is on a stage learning the technique of stopping to breathe under the direction of Kristina the facilitator. The other three students aren't around.

The stage is half-dark and without props with only black drop cloths on the two sides and in the back. The auditorium is completely dark and empty, so it appears to be a rehearsal rather than a performance.

Kristina the facilitator is dressed in a typical Wagnerian Brunhilde costume—a steel helmet with two cow horns on her head, a red cloak over her shoulders fastened with a golden clasp under her chin, a floor-long white robe, and an armor over her chest in the shape of two big shiny golden mixing bowls held in place by leather straps. She looks different too—tall and heavy with big blue eyes and thick long golden braids like the prototypical Wagnerian Brunhilde but there doesn't seem to be anything strange about it. She is the same Kristina the facilitator from real life.

RR has been told what to do and is trying to hold his breath. He has been doing it for a while because he is straining. His lips are tightly pressed together and his face is turning red. He won't be able to last much longer. Any second now he will breathe in.

Kristina the facilitator watches him and he knows she doesn't like what she sees. She has told him to relax and he is straining. He can see her face grow more and more red with anger and her eyes bulge out of her head. Any second now too she will scream.

She does this and he starts breathing at the same instant. He wasn't able to hold his breath any longer.

You idiot, she screams in a huge Wagnerian soprano voice, You're supposed to relax and here you're straining as if you were on a toilet. You're not squeezing anything out of your body. You're trying not to let the air come in. Make it so that you don't need it. You don't even have to close your mouth. You should just keep your chest from expanding.

Go ahead now, she says stepping up to him and putting her hands on his shoulders, Stand still, open your mouth, and don't breathe.

She looks even bigger than she did from farther away—she is looking straight into his eyes and is as tall as he.

RR does as he is told and stares back into Kristina the facilitator's eyes hoping this will help him. He wants to derive strength from her gaze.

At first it works and he feels great about having listened to her but after about ten seconds he starts feeling the need to breathe and begins to strain again. The effort gets harder and harder and even though he is keeping his mouth open he can still feel his face turn red. He hopes this will change but it keeps getting worse and he is sure any second now he will breathe in and so to prevent this he closes his mouth.

Kristina the facilitator gives out an even more ear-piercing Wagnerian soprano scream, No!, grabs him with one hand by his shoulder, turns him around, presses his head to the bowls on her chest so hard it hurts, and clasps her other hand tightly over his mouth while pinching his nose together with her thumb and index finger at the same time.

He does manage to take in a shallow breath as she is doing it however.

The air wasn't enough for him and so he wants to breathe in more but she is holding him firm and her hand is making it impossible for him to do this.

He is suffocating and struggles to free himself from her grip but she is too strong. Her arm is holding him like a vise against her chest, her hand is glued tight to his mouth, and her fingers hold his nostrils painfully together like a clamp.

He is desperate. He needs more air for he will suffocate. He can feel himself blacking out.

In a final outburst of despair he twists his body and almost manages to free himself but this causes her to loose her balance and they both fall backwards.

He still tries to pull her hand away from his face as they keep falling and finally is able to do it and at last breathes in. At the same instant he gives out the loudest scream he has ever made.

B. before the funeral

Kristina the student, Sophie, Walter the student, and RR in a room. They have just come back from Walter the facilitator's funeral.

The room small but with an abnormally tall ceiling that has a florid cornice running along three sides under it making it look like a piece cut off from a much bigger room (a ballroom). Peach-colored walls. No windows. A big chandelier hanging down from the ceiling making it look even more (certain?) it was part of a ballroom before. The chandelier all lit up making the contents of the room painfully clear.

Modernist furniture distributed haphazardly all over it as if for storage, to be removed soon, some items among it which normally stand against the wall at some distance away from one.

The furniture mostly from laminated light-colored wood with clear shellac over it, interesting complicated grain pattern showing through. Three-legged round-topped stools. Matching three-legged round-topped tables with black- or red-painted wooden tops. Narrow thin-armed armchairs with round backs upholstered in red or black oilcloth. Shallow wardrobes, chests of drawers, and dressers, some of the latter with mirrors attached to them. The mirrors rectangular, round, or oval.

Kristina the student squeezed into a red armchair leaning back in it, her arms and legs spread out with her heavy gray herringbone overcoat thrown over another red armchair not far on her left. Sophie still in her dark blue overcoat perched on top of a stool her hands clutched together her legs decorously turned to one side like a woman atop a horse in a ladies' saddle. Walter the student sitting up straight in a black armchair in his lumber jacket, jeans, and a black and white houndstooth flat cap on his head. RR in a black raincoat and umbrella in his hand standing up facing a rectangular mirror attached to a dresser as if looking out a window.

Kristina the student (*after a long silence, sitting up and glancing at the watch she wears on a chain on her neck under her shirt*): It's quarter after three.

Walter the student (*after checking his wristwatch without changing his position*): Three seventeen.

Kristina the student: I have three fourteen actually.

Sophie (*straightening out her knees and leaving them a shade apart while glancing at her wristwatch*): It's three twenty by my watch.

Kristina the student (*disdainfully*): You're always way off.

Sophie: Yes mine runs too fast. I have to reset it almost every day.

Kristina the student: You should take it to a watchmaker.

Sophie: I should but it's too much trouble.

Walter the student: I could fix it for you. It's not difficult. You just adjust the mechanism inside, that's all. I'll do it for you.

Sophie: Thanks. I'll give it to you later.

Walter the student: Good. It'll take a few seconds.... (*After a pause.*) As long as I don't have a problem opening the case. (*To Sophie, leaning over in her direction.*) Let me see it.

Sophie takes the watch off her wrist and leaning over gives it to Walter the student. He looks at it.

Walter the student (*handing the watch back to Sophie*): No, there'll be no problem. I have a knife that'll do it. Give it to me after dinner.

Sophie (*taking the watch*): I will. Thanks.

She puts the watch back on her wrist.

Kristina the student (*after about fifteen seconds of silence*): What time do you have RR?

RR (*turning partially away from the mirror and glancing at his wristwatch*): Three sixteen and (*Pauses.*) thirty seconds.

Kristina the student (*glances at her watch*): I have a little over three fifteen. (*After a pause.*) So you're about a minute faster than me. (*To Walter the student.*) And you....(*Hesitates.*)

Walter the student: I'm three minutes faster than you and Sophie six.

Kristina the student (*laughing*): Who cares about Sophie. Her watch is way off.

Sophie (*embarrassed, laughing nervously*): I'm sorry.

Kristina the student *(in mocked graciousness):* You're forgiven.

Silence follows.

Disturbed from his position RR turns completely away from the mirror and starts pacing back and forth diagonally across the room. He swings his umbrella as he walks.

After a few minutes Walter the student gets up and does the same except along the other diagonal. The two men adjust their pace so as not to collide when they cross each other's path.

Kristina the student leans back and wiggles herself into a more comfortable position in the tight armchair without throwing her arms and legs wide apart however. Seeing what Kristina the student has done Sophie also makes herself more comfortable on her stool keeping her knees decorous once again except leaning the other way.

The two women silently watch the two men move pendulum-like through the room.

14. the en

a room, a cube, a three-dimensional space enclosed by three pairs

of rectangles of   different dimensions, a cube, a room, a

no windows, walls, just walls, just no windows, no

the walls dark, dark green, black, green black, black green, green

black, the walls, the

the room dark, not black, just dark, just dark the room, dark, the,

just

cables hanging down from the ceiling, wires, tubes, veins, entrails,

tubes, cables, hanging, down

sheets hanging down from the ceiling, sheets of cloth, of plastic,

of blood, of white blood, aurora borealis, of cloth, of

plastic, of white blood, of

in the middle a stand, a tall stand, a tall bed, a flat tall bed, a

catafalque, a dining room table, a kitchen table, an

operating table, a tall bed, a hospital bed, a

on the stand, table, bed he, he on, on the, he, the, on

from afar voices, far voices from afar, of people, of patients, of
    loved ones, of hospital staff, of, from far afar, of from

a single voice from high above on the right, from above high,
    from the outside, from the inside, an inner voice from
    above on the right, from outside, a strong outside inner
    voice from

stretch out your body, limbs, arms, legs, all, all, stretch out,
    stretch, stretch, stretch, stretch out, yes, that's it, now
    you're good, you're fine

lie still now, lie still, still, still, still stiller, still stiller, stiller, stiller,
    still, still, still, yes, there you are, that's it, you're still
    now, now you're good, you're fine

now close your eyes, eyelids, eyelids parallel to arms and legs,
    eyelids parallel to parallel lines, to lines intersecting at
    infinity, eyelids parallel, parallel, parallel, eyes
    perpendicular, eyes perpendicular to lines, perpendicular
    to infinity, eyes perpendicular to blackness, eyes to
    blackness, eyes to blackness, eyes to blackness, yes, that's
    it, good, yes, now you're good, you're fine

give me some color now, some color, white color, white color,

    white, white, white, gray color now, grey color, more gray

    color, more gray, more gray, enough gray color now,

    enough gray, more white color now, more white, more

    white, too much white now, too much white color, more

    gray, more gray color, more gray, more gray, gray, gray,

    yes, that's it, now you're good, you're fine

stop breathing now, stop breathing, stop, stop, stop, stop, just a

    little more, a little more, stop, stop, stop, that's it, there

    you are, now yes, now you're good, you're

fin

synopsis

The themes of alienation, abandonment, and fear of death, developed in *Like Blood in Water* and elaborated in *The Future of Giraffes*, respectively the first and second book of *The Placebo Effect Trilogy*, are picked up in the third book, *View of Delft*, and are given a new treatment in German context. A neurotic intellectual lets himself be adopted by a couple with a Down syndrome son to escape the stress of being normal. Another man searches desperately for a meaning in life to become mad in the end. The son of a suicidal Prussian Junker family becomes obsessed with an albino boy, thinking he has caused his death. Love between two people is shown to be as transient as a cloud. And a traveler accidentally finds himself in a hospital/boarding school where they teach the residents how to die.

The five mininovels that make up *View of Delft*, as is the case with its two companions, all employ *negative text*—gaps of vital information which the reader is obliged to supply himself. By bringing personal experience into the story, the reader makes it more vivid and real, becoming in the process its co-author together with the author of the text.

biography

Yuriy Tarnawsky has authored more than two dozen books of poetry, fiction, drama, essays, and translations. He was born in Ukraine but raised and educated in the West. An engineer and linguist by training, he has worked as a computer scientist at IBM Corporation and professor of Ukrainian literature and culture at Columbia University. He writes in Ukrainian and English and resides in the New York City area.

His other English-language books include the books of fiction *Meningitis*, *Three Blondes and Death*, *Like Blood in Water* (all FC2), *Short Tails*, and *The Future of Giraffes* (both JEF Books), as well as the play *Not Medea* (JEF).

Great Works of Innovative Fiction Published by JEF Books

Collected Stort Shories by Erik Belgum
Oppression for the Heaven of It by Moore Bowen [2013 Patchen
       Award!]
Don't Sing Aloha When I Go by Robert Casella
How to Break Article Noun by Carolyn Chun [2012 Patchen
       Award!]
What Is Art? by Norman Conquest
Elder Physics by James R. Hugunin
Something Is Crook in Middlebrook by James R. Hugunin [2012 *Zoom
       Street* Experimental Fiction Book of the Year!]
OD: Docufictions by Harold Jaffe
Paris 60 by Harold Jaffe
Apostrophe/Parenthesis by Frederick Mark Kramer
Ambiguity by Frederick Mark Kramer
Minnows by Jønathan Lyons
You Are Make Very Important Bathtime by David Moscovich
Xanthous Mermaid Mechanics by Brion Poloncic
Short Tails by Yuriy Tarnawsky
The Placebo Effect Trilogy by Yuriy Tarnawsky
Prism and Graded Monotony by Dominic Ward

For a complete listing of all our titles
please visit us at experimentalfiction.com

CPSIA information can be obtained at www.ICGtesting.com
Printed in the USA
LVOW10s0043121114

413137LV00024B/856/P